Watching that hazy blob on the screen come to life brought up so many emotions he had to swallow down before he started wailing.

It should have been such an exciting time seeing his baby for the first time, but this was the second time he'd been here. The memories of sitting here holding Janet's hand were too painful for him to enjoy the moment even when the heartbeat sounded out around the room to let them know everything was all right.

Then he noticed the frown on the sonographer's face and the quick movement of the doppler farther over Izzy's stomach. She hadn't missed it either.

"What's wrong? I thought the baby was okay?" Her eyes were wide with panic and she almost cut off the circulation in his fingers with her grip. Cal's own breath stilled as they waited for a reply.

"You haven't had your twelve-week scan yet?"

Izzy shook her head.

"What? What is it?" It was Cal's turn to voice his concern.

"I was confirming a healthy heartbeat, but I've found more than one. Meet baby number two." She turned the screen around so they could see the evidence for themselves.

Dear Reader,

I admire everyone who works for the emergency services, and the air ambulance crew are a recent addition to the medical staff here in Northern Ireland. It must be an exhilarating and rewarding job to go up in that helicopter every day but also a dangerous one. I imagine those are very special people dedicated to saving others who put their patients' safety well above their own.

There was no doubt in my mind when writing this story that my Northern Irish paramedic, Isobel Fitzpatrick, would be a fiery redhead, too stubborn to realize she doesn't have to do everything on her own. Of course, this means she needs the calming influence of sexy doctor Cal Armstrong, who has been her best friend since training.

I love a good friends-to-lovers story, watching the relationship between characters develop over time. Izzy and Cal's situation throws them in at the deep end after both are just coming out of bad relationships, so their emotions take some unraveling!

I hope you enjoy the journey with them, but make sure to strap yourself in for a bumpy ride.

Happy Reading!

Karin xx

THEIR ONE-NIGHT
TWIN SURPRISE

—

KARIN BAINE

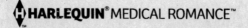

HARLEQUIN® MEDICAL ROMANCE™

Recycling programs
for this product may
not exist in your area.

ISBN-13: 978-1-335-64174-8

Their One-Night Twin Surprise

First North American Publication 2019

Copyright © 2019 by Karin Baine

Printed in U.S.A.

For Jane xx

Praise for
Karin Baine

PROLOGUE

Izzy Fitzpatrick ran blindly out into the night, uncaring about the rain soaking through her clothes and bringing goose-bumps out over her skin. She didn't know where she was going, only that she no longer felt safe in her own home. Her whole life as she knew it seemed to have unravelled completely over the course of the evening.

It was bad enough she was still mourning the loss of the man she'd thought she was going to marry and raise her much-longed-for family with, but to discover Gerry had sold her a lie all along was something she knew she'd never recover from.

Now she needed to be somewhere she felt protected, be with someone she could trust. It was no wonder she found herself standing outside Cal Armstrong's house. He was her friend, her colleague, and a man she knew she could turn to in a crisis.

She jabbed at the buzzer on the gate, desperate to get inside and close the door on the nightmare haunting her out here.

Eventually the voice of a sleepy-sounding Cal came over the intercom. 'Hello?'

'Cal?' The sheer relief of hearing his familiar voice was enough to completely break her and the dam broke on the tears she'd been trying to hold at bay with every revelation she'd uncovered tonight.

'Izzy, is that you? What's wrong? I'm coming down.' The gates swung open and she ran towards the house as though she was still being chased by Gerry's invisible demons.

He was pulling on a T-shirt as he opened the door and Izzy launched herself at him, making him stagger backwards into the hall. 'Oh, Cal, I didn't know where else to go, who else to turn to.'

'Calm down and tell me what's wrong. You're safe now.' He kicked the door closed behind her and she was inclined to believe him. His solid presence was just the reassurance she needed right now.

She let him hold her, enjoying being co-cooned in his strong arms and the heat of his body warming hers as the cold reality of Gerry's betrayal hit home.

'There was a man at the house…he said Gerry owed him money…something to do with a card game.' Her teeth were chattering now with the shock of having a visit from the kind of people she'd thought only existed in gangster movies.

'Did he hurt you?' Cal tensed beneath her, his biceps bunching and flexing as he demanded the truth.

'No. He was just…intimidating. I told him about the accident, that Gerry had been killed, but he didn't seem to care. He wanted the debt paid. I had to give him every penny I had in the house to make him leave.' She shivered, remembering Gerry's associate standing with a foot inside her door, knowing she was there alone and terrified he'd want more than cash from her.

Cal swore and pulled her tighter into his embrace. 'You're freezing and soaking wet. Go inside and get warm by the fire. I'll get you some towels and warm clothes.'

He led her into the living room, put a blanket around her shoulders and handed her a glass of amber liquid. 'For the shock,' he said, making her drink it before he went to get her the dry clothes he'd promised.

Her throat burned as she downed the alcohol, but she was grateful as it took the chill from her very bones and warmed her from the inside out. That unpleasant house call had only been the start of unravelling Gerry's secrets and lies and now she was afraid there could be a string of debtors turning up on her doorstep looking for recompense.

'I'm sorry I didn't have more in your size,' he said with a half-grin and she appreciated he was still trying to make her laugh even at a time like this. She needed Cal's stability, this normality, to prevent her from tipping completely over the edge.

'That's fine. Thank you.' Izzy took the fresh towels and Cal-sized outfit from him, but she didn't have the energy, or the inclination, to leave the room to get changed. She simply sat and stared at the pile of laundry on her lap, unable to move.

'Let me.' Cal knelt at her feet and gently tugged off her shoes and socks, followed by her sodden trousers and blouse. He moved swiftly and efficiently to strip her of her wet things, leaving just her underwear before wrapping her in a warm, fluffy robe.

He took one of the towels, sat beside her on the sofa and began to dry her hair. She closed her eyes as he massaged her scalp, finding comfort in the intimate gesture. It had been a long time, if ever, since anyone had done that for her.

'I'm sorry for imposing on you like this. I know I'm making a habit of turning up here unannounced.'

'There's no need to apologise and as for your previous visits, I think they were more of an intervention for my benefit. If I hadn't had you chivvying me along after Janet left me I'd either still be in bed, unable to face the world again, or in rehab for jilted men whose fiancées had run off with the *actual* fathers of their babies.' Cal's dark humour failed to disguise how much Janet had really hurt him by stringing him along, pretending they were going to have a baby together.

Izzy understood his pain more than ever since Gerry had essentially done the same thing to her. He'd promised to marry her one day and give her the family she'd always dreamed of but that would never have happened.

'Well, if we're playing who had the worst relationship, I'll see your lying fiancée and raise you a gambling addict.' That was the only way she could see him now, tonight's revelations overriding everything she'd thought she knew about Gerry.

Cal's soothing hands stilled on her scalp. 'Oh, Izzy. I'm so sorry.'

She shrugged but the tears made a resurgence as she thought of all her hopes and dreams for the future that had been doomed from the first time they'd met. 'I've been mourning him for two months, but I wasted my grief on a stranger. That knock on the door tonight prompted me to finally look at all the post and paperwork he left behind. He'd taken out bank loans in my name, forged my signature on goodness knows what and racked up debt wherever he went. It's going to take ages to sort through the mess he's left behind. I just feel so alone, Cal.'

With no family to turn to and her best friend, Helen, living miles away, those old feelings of rejection were surfacing again.

She was lucky she had Cal to lend her a shoulder to lean on.

'You're not alone. I'm here for you, day or night, the way you were for me.' He put his arms around her neck and kissed the top of her head.

'What did we do to deserve Janet and Gerry?' Izzy had seen him in the depths of despair where she was currently languishing, and it just didn't seem fair.

'Absolutely nothing.' He tipped her face up and made her look at him. 'None of this is your fault. Okay?'

'I remember saying something similar to you not so long ago…' Somehow just being in Cal's company was enough for her to stop panicking and provide her with some comfort. She hoped she'd managed the same for him in the aftermath of Janet's departure, even though turning up, unwanted, with home-cooked meals and taking the beer out of his hands had seemed like a thankless task at the time.

'Well, I think I needed reminding then and now so do you. You're a good person, Izzy.' Izzy snuggled into the crook of his arm, gazing into his eyes and realising how special he really was.

She'd never looked at him in a romantic way before but now, wrapped in his embrace, her body was responding to him altogether differently from what she was used to. The comfort she'd found with him had turned into something new and thrilling, desire stealthily making itself known so she was aware of every spot where his body was pressed against hers, that tingling sensation electrifying every inch of her skin.

He was looking at her now with the same hunger in his eyes as she was currently experiencing and the atmosphere between them was suddenly crackling with sexual tension.

She tilted her head up to his, stopped when she thought it might be an unwanted advance, then rejoiced when he bent to meet her lips with his.

They sealed the strange new dynamic with an exploratory kiss that soon obliterated Izzy's doubts that he might only be offering her comfort. She could tell from the increased passionate intensity of his kisses that Cal wanted her as much as she wanted him at that moment. Their mouths were clashing together, they were tugging at each other's clothes in their frantic need to make that ultimate connection, and Izzy knew things between them would never be the same again.

CHAPTER ONE

Three months later

THE MINUTE THE call came in Izzy knew it was going to be a tough one for her.

'We have a thirty-one-year-old pregnant woman badly hurt after a car accidentally reversed through a shop window.' She paused to clear her throat before she continued relaying the harrowing details to the rest of the crew on board the air ambulance. 'The patient was shunted through the glass and has suffered severe lacerations and potential crush injuries. Her wrist and main artery have been severed but police on the scene have applied a tourniquet to her arm and require immediate medical assistance.'

'What about the driver of the car?' Cal's voice came over the headset and she knew, as the attending doctor, he was concerned for everybody's safety at the scene.

'Superficial injuries and shock, as far as we can tell. The ambulance can take him to hospital by road, but time is of the essence for our pregnant lady.' Depending on how much blood she'd lost and how long it took for them to get her to the hospital, there was a chance both mother and baby might not make it. Unfortunately, death was a part of the job but under current circumstances this one felt a bit close to home when Izzy's hormones were already all over the place.

Once the pilot found a clear place to land they hurried towards the melee of people and flashing lights. Thankfully the police had cordoned off the area so they could get to work without interference from the general public who were watching the drama unfold.

'This is Tara Macready. She's four months pregnant and has sustained substantial wounds to her left arm. We've been applying pressure to the wound since we arrived on scene.' One of the young police officers talked them through events as his colleagues did their best to stop the patient bleeding out. With their first-aid training they'd known to elevate the arm and apply pressure to reduce the flow of blood and had probably saved her life in the process. They'd done their part and now it was up to Izzy and Cal to get her transferred to the hospital as soon as possible.

Despite the police officers' good work, the ground was heavily stained with the scarlet evidence of the patient's trauma and Izzy had to fight against the unexpected emotions welling up inside her. 'Tara, we're with the air ambulance crew. We're going to take over now and get you transferred to the hospital.'

'What about my baby?' she mumbled, battling against unconsciousness.

'We're going to monitor you both, but we need to do a few things first, Tara. Izzy, she needs a bilateral cannula as quick as you can.' Cal set to work getting a pressure bandage on to replace the makeshift tourniquet that had been applied to Tara's arm and Izzy inserted the cannula so they could administer fluids. Once she was at the hospital they could do the blood typing necessary for a transfusion.

'I'm giving you some morphine for the pain, Tara.' With the bleeding halted Cal went ahead with pain relief. In this situation, even though they wanted to save both lives, the mother took priority.

Their portable kit enabled them to monitor Tara's blood pressure and heart rate and Izzy made sure everything was in place before they transferred her to the helicopter. They both climbed into the back with their patient so they could keep a close eye on her for the duration of the flight.

'I'm going to take a listen to your baby while the doctor checks your progress. Okay, Tara?' Izzy kept talking her through what was happening, reassuring her everything was going to be all right, even though she was slipping in and out of consciousness.

With a special stethoscope she was able to put her ear down to Tara's belly and listen for the baby's heartbeat. Hearing that faint rhythm felt like winning the lottery and Cal mirrored her smile when he realised the baby was still hanging in there too.

'Your baby is fighting right along with you, Tara. We'll get you both to the hospital as quickly as we can.' It was all down to timing now and Izzy was taking this one more personally than anything she'd ever witnessed before. Apparently, the prospect of becoming a mother made a woman fight harder than ever and that was one symptom of pregnancy she could get on board with.

Izzy could have kissed the tarmac when the helicopter touched down back at their Belfast base after transferring their patient into the hands of the emergency staff at the hospital.

'Are you okay, Fizz? You're looking a little green around the gills there. Don't tell me you've developed a sudden fear of flying? We'd have to ground you and then who would I have to wind up on a daily basis?'

She rolled her eyes at a grinning Cal. He knew she hated that nickname he'd foisted on her when they'd first met at air ambulance training and she'd let her temper get the better of her, striving to prove she was better than any of the men there.

At least, she used to hate it. In the five years of working together it had grown on her and she'd missed it of late when things between them had become awkward, to say the least. Things weren't going to get any easier between them once he heard her news.

They'd both been hurt by people who'd

purported to love them. Cal's pregnant fiancée, Janet, had run out on him with the man who was apparently the *real* father of the baby she was carrying, leaving double the void in his life and double the hurt.

Izzy knew the heart-stabbing pain of betrayal, thanks to Gerry, the man she'd thought she'd spend the rest of her life with. She'd put all her hopes and dreams into their relationship, believing he was the one who was going to give her the family and stability she'd never had growing up in the foster system, only to have everything cruelly snatched away from her when he'd been killed in a motorcycle accident.

The only thing worse than losing someone she loved had been discovering he hadn't been who she'd thought he was at all. A parade of nefarious debt collectors and loan sharks who'd bankrolled a gambling addiction she'd been oblivious to and a bank account emptied as a result of his addiction had merely fuelled the notion that she would never have anyone in her life who loved her unconditionally. The realisation that had sent her running to the one person in her life she knew she could trust.

In Cal she'd found a kindred, wounded soul and she'd needed him to comfort her. They'd shared that one incredible night together but they both knew it could never be more than that when they were too raw to even think of getting involved in any sort of relationship. It was difficult enough going back to work as though nothing had happened between them when every erotic memory of sharing his bed was still so vivid in her mind.

And that one night of seeking solace in Cal's arms had ended in the life-changing consequences she was yet to tell him about. She didn't know how he was going to react to the news he was going to become a father so soon after his break-up and, to be truthful, she didn't want to lose his friendship if he resented the fact she was pregnant with his baby instead of Janet.

'I'm perfectly fine,' she bristled, as they ducked under the still spinning blades of the air ambulance.

This pregnancy might have come as a shock, but she wasn't going to let it get in the way of doing her job. The time would come soon enough when her bump would encroach on the limited space inside the chopper and prevent her from being as physically involved in the rescues as she was used to. At which point in time she'd probably have to become more involved in ground operations and hospital transfers, but not before then.

She was sure the odd bout of nausea would pass soon now she was reaching the end of her first trimester. Although she'd been unaware of the little person growing inside her belly for most of that time. Since she and Cal had agreed to put their indiscretion behind them, it hadn't entered her head that she might be pregnant and had blamed the stress of finding out about Gerry's secret vice as the cause for her missed period. Now everything was going to change between them.

Those tears, which never seemed far away, blurred her vision once more and she rested her hand on the slight swell of her belly to reassure her little bean it still had her, even if Cal decided he didn't want to be involved. She needed to confide in someone and the closest she had to family was Helen, her childhood friend and the only person she'd had growing up who had seemed to genuinely care for her.

Helen still lived in the Donegal area, where Izzy had spent the last of her teenage years before moving to Belfast to study nursing. She was a shoulder for Izzy to lean on when she needed one and though there was a vast geographical distance between them, hearing her voice would be enough to comfort her. Once she got over the shock herself, Izzy resolved to make that phone call. There was just one other person she had to inform first.

'Seriously, though, are you sure you're all right?' Cal stepped closer, his frown wiping away all traces of joviality, his pale blue eyes full of concern.

Izzy dropped her hand, so he wouldn't guess her secret.

'Low blood sugar, I expect. I haven't eaten all day.' A complete lie. Her blood was probably ninety per cent sugar due to the number of biscuits she'd been wolfing down lately.

'Why didn't you say? I'm sure we can do better than a cup of tea and a stale bun in the canteen. After what we've just been through we could probably do with something a lot stronger. Pub?' He began to unzip his bright orange flight suit and let the sleeves drop to his waist, revealing the lean frame encased in a tight black T-shirt beneath the bulky protective layers.

Izzy told herself it was pregnancy hormones making it impossible for her to drag her eyes away. That was the bonus side of her condition, being able to blame recent impulses, including an apparent spike in her libido, on the changes going on inside her body. Although her intimate knowledge of that hard body and the pleasures it could bring a woman was making her temperature rise steadily with every flashback of that night they'd spent together.

It was a loss to womankind that because one of their sisters had been blind to what a great man he was, all the rest would be denied the privilege of getting close to him. Except her, of course, but then they'd agreed it would never happen again, no matter how physically compatible they'd turned out to be. It was ironic that they hadn't wanted to complicate their relationship by getting romantically involved when they were now going to be tied together for the rest of their lives.

Izzy watched him climb out of his suit and flash her that cheeky grin of his.

'Enjoying the view?'

'You wish,' she shot back with just as much sarcasm before he realised how true his observation had been.

Given the physical nature of their work, it was important to keep up their fitness levels, but Cal was the type who could never sit still anyway. His trim, nicely muscled physique wasn't the result of hours spent at the gym. He wasn't the slightest bit vain enough to spend time staring at himself in the mirror whilst he hoisted weights. No, this perfect specimen of the male anatomy was a pleasant result of his busy life as a doctor in the field and the manual labour he did in his vast garden in his spare time.

She shivered as some particularly erotic memories sprang to mind of this handsome man with his tan, sun-bleached mop of hair and that mischievous glint in his eye, lying naked next to her.

'Are you sure you're all right? You've got that hungry look in your eyes again.'

Izzy blinked away inappropriate thoughts and images of her colleague, her friend, and the one constant she'd had in her life here in Belfast before she'd screwed up and potentially lost him for ever too.

'Just starved.' Apparently for more than food. Not that he'd ever shown any interest in her as a woman apart from as another one of his mates until that night.

It hadn't been planned. Izzy had just needed to be with someone who cared about her. Through the tears and shared stories of heartbreak they'd found themselves kissing and searching for some feeling of peace. She didn't regret anything. It had been a beautifully raw expression of their affection and compassion for one another. They simply should have taken adequate precautions for their evening as friends with benefits.

'Let me get the paperwork out of the way and we'll head to the pub before you get hangry. I know what you're like when you're so hungry you turn into a red-headed hulk.'

If she'd had any doubts that he only saw her as a mate, they vanished. She was so completely friend zoned he didn't expect her to take offence at that comment.

'Do not,' she huffed, regardless she knew very well her fiery temper reached boiling point when there was a lack of food close to hand. He hadn't drawn a pretty picture of her when she'd created a sexy centrefold out of him. 'I'm not keen on the pub idea either.'

She worried he'd be suspicious if she sat in the bar nursing an orange juice instead of her usual glass of wine.

'Dinner at that new Italian place, then? Although it'll probably mean having to go home and get changed first. I'm not sure sweaty work clothes will fit their dress code.' He was being unnecessarily concerned. Cal always managed to smell amazing no matter how stressful their shift proved or how energetic he'd been.

'Hmm, I fancy something stodgy and greasy.' She didn't.

'I'll die of starvation if you make me go home first.' She wouldn't. However, if they went to that posh place and Cal changed the habit of a lifetime by not offering to pay the entire bill she'd be mortified because she couldn't afford it.

Even before she'd discovered there'd be a new mouth to feed in the future, she'd been struggling to cover the bills. Gerry had never officially moved in, but he'd used her place as a base when not travelling around the country as a pharmaceutical rep. It wasn't that she was missing his financial contributions to household expenses, quite the opposite. He was the reason she had no savings left to furnish her nest now.

She'd invited him into her heart and her home without the knowledge of his gambling habits. Gerry had had no family or friends either to call on for help and the cost of his funeral on top of his other financial mismanagement meant money was tight for her and nothing short of a miracle would change that now. Wages would have to stretch as far as possible and that would mean cutting back on luxuries like fancy Italian restaurants or any sort of social life.

Izzy should have known better than to think she was sitting pretty at any stage of her life and keep herself protected. Being a kid bounced around the care system had taught her never to rely on anyone except herself and never to let her guard down. Once too often she'd imagined she'd found her forever home, only to be returned like an ill-fitting shirt. Too young, too old, too opinionated, too red, she'd been a nineties

Anne Shirley, without the lovable Matthew and Marilla Cuthbert giving her a happy ending at Green Gables.

Meals and board had been provided along with whatever basic material possessions she'd needed, but that all-important element had been missing, as it had for most of her life. Love wasn't something given or received easily for her, even with Gerry.

It had been a slow burn for them but eventually she'd learned to trust, to open up her heart and believe him when he'd promised her a future and a family together.

Even though Cal knew about Gerry's betrayal since it was the reason she'd been driven to his arms, the extent of her financial struggles was another secret she was keeping from someone she considered a friend. With good reason. He'd insist on riding in on his white steed, waving his fat wallet, to save her and she wasn't going to be indebted to him or anyone else. She had to get used to managing on her own when she had errands to run or do the night feeds when she was exhausted beyond belief. The stakes were too high now for her to let anyone into that armoured heart again.

'The "caff" it is, then.' Cal took the lead from Izzy's clues as to what she could afford, not necessarily what she craved. Which, at this moment, didn't go beyond a chance to kick off her shoes and sit down with a cup of builder's tea.

'Do you think they're going to be okay?' Izzy cradled the chipped mug in her hands, drawing comfort from the heat as a chill fluttered over her skin.

'Who?' Cal sawed off another chunk of sausage and popped it into his mouth. It had become a tradition to go for a meal when their shift had ended. Not only because they'd worked up an appetite, but they needed that time to come down from the adrenaline high and process what they'd gone through at the scene of whatever medical emergency they'd just attended.

'Tara Macready and her baby—you know, the woman we just saved.' She set her tea down and poked the sausage and bacon on her plate with a fork. A fry-up was the standard fare in this particular establishment, but the smell of grease was making her feel queasy again. Rather than make him suspicious she'd ordered her usual, but she'd only managed to nibble at the toast so far.

'We did our best and they're in the best place to recover.' Cal carried on eating, but the image of the blood and knowledge of Tara's condition wouldn't leave her. Most people probably wouldn't have realised she was pregnant, but Izzy would've noticed even if it hadn't been in her notes. These days she was aware of every new change in her body and she'd recognised Tara had the same slightly swollen belly as she did.

This kind of accident wasn't an unusual sight, given the nature of their work, and it was vital they kept a certain detachment when attending these scenes. They weren't supposed to take the emotional trauma home with them and usually she didn't, other than a phone call to check up on a patient's progress.

This one was different as it was a mother and her unborn child in jeopardy. Perhaps they'd all be different now she was going to be a mother herself. The idea of setting off in the helicopter alone was making her question her own mortality these days. Until now she'd never worried about her own safety up there, but in the not-too-distant future she was going to have someone depending on her coming home from work day after day.

The sound of cutlery clattering onto the plate made her jump and the touch of Cal's hand as he settled it on hers didn't help soothe her nerves.

'They would never have made it at all if they'd gone by road and she might lose the use of her hand but they're still alive. Now, are you going to tell me what's going on in that head of yours today? You're not yourself at all.' It wasn't that Cal didn't have sympathy for them, but he knew, as well as she did, that they had to do their job and move onto the next one without looking back in case it affected future call-outs.

That had taken some getting used to, although she'd had years of experience as a nurse in A and E. Cal too, a consultant in emergency medicine, had found those first cases difficult to walk away from at the hospital doors. They'd often talked into the wee hours about their day, much to his fiancée's annoyance.

These pregnancy hormones were making her feel as though she'd taken a step back, seeing everything in a new, terrifying light. Not that she had any intention of giving up her job. She loved being part of the team being whisked up into the air at a moment's notice to save people in trouble. This was simply a blip and one she couldn't wait to get over, along with this nausea.

'Sorry. I'm not the best company at the minute.'

He squeezed her hand. 'You know I'm here for you anytime.'

His misplaced concern caused her eyes to prickle with tears. Recently she'd suspected her eyeballs had been replaced by tiny hedgehogs, that was happening so often. He was so considerate it pained her, knowing she was about to turn his world on its head again.

'Thanks,' she said, withdrawing her hand from the safety of his. It wasn't going to do her any good to expect Cal to prop her up every time she had a wobble, no matter how comforting it was. They hadn't planned this baby and whilst she was reconciled some way to the idea of becoming a parent there was no guarantee he would. There was every chance she would end up raising their child alone and she was fine with that. If that's what Cal wanted.

'Perhaps you came back too early—you know, after Gerry,' he said softly with some hesitation, and she knew he was half expecting her to kick off at the suggestion. Which she usually did when anyone tried to tell her what to do, thinking they knew her better than she knew herself.

She didn't agree with him on this occasion either but she'd no other way to explain her current mood without spilling the beans about the baby.

'You could be right.' She pushed her plate away before she vomited.

Now Cal knew something really was wrong with Izzy. She usually fought him over the smallest difference of opinion, so daring to suggest something as huge as she'd returned to work too soon warranted all-out war.

Between that and her roller-coaster appetite he was beginning to worry about her. One minute she was eating everything in sight, including his emergency chocolate stash he kept for those occasions they didn't have time for a meal break. The next she was sitting staring at her rejected fry-up as though she was about to burst into tears at any second.

He hadn't noticed until today how emotional she'd become, having taken her stoicism and ability to bounce back from any eventuality for granted. Caught up in the sorrow of his own break-up, he hadn't seen past the front she'd been putting on since Gerry had died, accepting her assurances she was fine too easily. Probably because he didn't want to over-analyse what had happened between them that night when she'd come to his place in a state about Gerry.

He'd been committed to his relationship with Janet, even if she hadn't considered it a priority, but when Izzy had come to him seeking support and comfort, any thoughts of his ex had been obliterated by his all-consuming need for her. Once he'd tasted desire on her lips, all those suppressed feelings he'd apparently been harbouring for her had been tangled in there right along with their limbs and tongues. He never considered that she might've been down in those depths of despair all this time.

Yes, Janet had betrayed him in the worst

possible way, stringing him along with that dream of his happy family, only to snatch it away for ever. It had been partly his fault, so desperate to set up a loving home like the one he'd grown up in he'd clung onto the wrong person, ignoring all her flaws in favour of the family he'd envisaged having with her. Now he was worried he'd taken advantage of Izzy when she was obviously still emotionally vulnerable.

They'd been close for years and that bond had irritated their partners at times, but they'd only crossed the line that night when their relationships had forcibly ended. Ever since they'd fallen into bed together he'd found it difficult to rein those feelings back in and pretend nothing had happened. They'd agreed that was the best course of action, but it was impossible to put their indiscretion completely out of his head when he saw her every day and was reminded how incredible that time together had been. As though they'd finally stopped pretending their chemistry was nothing more than camaraderie and had expressed their feelings for one another physically.

How was he supposed to forget something

so amazingly honest after his recent experience of deceit?

'I've been a bad friend to you lately. I'm sorry.' There'd been a distance between them recently, which he'd created as a coping mechanism to protect himself, never thinking about the support Izzy needed. He thought back over these past horrendous months and thought of all the support she'd offered him after Janet had left.

Izzy had been a constant on his doorstep despite his repeated warnings he didn't want to see or talk to anyone in the aftermath of his ex's revelation. She'd been the provider of home-cooked meals when he hadn't wanted to eat and the confiscator of alcohol when all he'd wanted to do was drink. Ignoring his bad temper, she'd fought past his defences and dragged him out of the quagmire, so he'd been able to get on with his life when he'd truly believed it was over.

That was the true definition of a friend. Not someone who muttered his sympathies and accepted her grieving was over because it suited him better than having to dig beyond a fake smile and talk about feelings. Now, seeing her here, eyes glassy with unshed tears, biting her lip to keep up the façade, he wanted to finally step up and be there for her. The way she'd done for him. She was the closest thing he had to family now. The only one who'd been there with him through the darkest hours of his life, and he owed her.

'Don't be daft. Aren't you here, putting up with my mood swings?' There was that smile again that he was learning not to trust when her eyes were cloudy with uncertainty and something else he couldn't quite decipher but which made him feel guiltier than ever.

'I wasn't there for you after Gerry died.'

'Um, I think you were.'

He wasn't expecting her to reference what had happened between them but there was a suggestion of that passionate encounter flickering like erotic flames in her eyes. Rather than complicate matters more between them, Cal chose to ignore the reminder. In conversation at least. 'If something's wrong I expect you to tell me and let me help. Okay?'

'Understood. Now, shall we get the bill?' She wrestled out from his grip and waved to the waitress.

Cal sighed and pulled his credit card from his wallet. 'I'll get this. It's the least I can do.'

Izzy made her usual protests as she fished in her bag for her purse, but he grabbed the bill first. 'Let me pay my half at least.'

'You can leave a couple of pounds for the tip if you want.' It was then he caught a glimpse inside her purse to see only a few coppers resting in the lining. Rather than embarrass her further, he tossed the loose change he found in his pocket on the table and made to leave.

Something wasn't right with Izzy and he wasn't going to rest until he discovered what. And if he wasn't the friend she needed he knew how to find the one who fitted that description.

CHAPTER TWO

'THIS IS SUPPOSED to be fun,' Cal called back to Izzy, who was doubled over trying to get her breath back and looking as though she was hating every second of this.

'I'm sure you're enjoying yourself, but I'd rather be vegging out watching the telly on my day off.' Izzy straightened up, pulled a hairband out of her pocket and tied her wild mane of red hair away from her face. Despite her protests, he thought she looked happier than she had in days, hiking out here in the County Down countryside, in the shadow of the Mourne Mountains. To be on the safe side he'd contacted Helen, who she often talked about, and suggested she might want to check in with her friend. It hadn't been difficult to make contact when Helen's phone number was on the birth announcement she'd sent Izzy after her son was born. The picture of mother and baby with the time and date of arrival took pride of place on Izzy's desk at work.

'I think we've both done our fair share of moping around. The fresh air will do you good.' He'd been keeping a closer eye on her lately and had noticed how withdrawn she seemed to have become compared to the old, devil-may-care Fizz he'd come to know.

There was always some excuse post-shift now about why she couldn't come out for a meal or even a quick drink, and he hated to think of her shut away in that empty house with nothing but memories to keep her company. After Janet had left him he'd thought he'd never venture over the doorstep again, afraid to face the world outside. Izzy had gone through a lot and was bound to have been changed by it, but he was determined not to let her retreat from civilisation altogether.

Since she didn't seem keen on spending time in crowded places he'd gone to the other extreme and dragged her out on one of his walks in the countryside with him.

'You can sit still and enjoy the fresh air. I think they call it sunbathing.'

'With your colouring?' He snorted as she tried to convince him her pale skin did anything other than freckle and burn.

Izzy shrugged off her jacket and tied it around her waist. Although he'd been concerned she wasn't eating properly, as her white T-shirt drew taut he could see she'd filled out a bit over these past weeks. He was glad. She looked better with a little meat on her bones, healthier, and as the sun shone through her shirt, silhouetting her figure, he could see exactly which parts of her had blossomed.

'Enjoying the view?' An amused Izzy echoed the words he'd teased her with the other day and snapped Cal's attention away from the soft round breasts he so clearly remembered palming in his hands.

'I was doing this for your benefit. I prefer a hike in the mountains myself.' He dismissed her comment, instead of confirming where his gaze had been lingering.

This walk was small potatoes for him when he preferred the challenge of a hill climb, whatever the weather, where he was focused on every step lest he end up at the bottom of a ravine. It was good for him to keep busy, his mind and body too active to entertain thoughts of his broken dreams, and he wanted to do the same for her.

'Yeah, 'cause we don't see enough of this at work.' Izzy rolled her eyes and started walking again.

'Who could ever tire of this?' He held his arms aloft in celebration of today's beautiful blue skies. They weren't always blessed with such favourable weather in Northern Ireland, even during these summer months, and he was of the opinion they should enjoy every second before the rain made another appearance.

'Me. Pretty. Damn. Quickly,' she huffed out as she climbed the slight incline of the bluebell-lined pathway, her slim legs flexing below her shorts with every step.

Cal let her reach the top first, determined to see her do this at her own pace in case he scared her off altogether. Today was about re-forging that bond between them so she'd be comfortable enough to share what was really going on in her life now, without any awkwardness coming between them.

She stood above him, hands on hips, face tilted towards the sky, eyes closed and soaking up the heat of the sun. This was what he wanted for her, to find peace and be free of the stresses she was under. Studying her from here, he could see why his ex had always seemed so threatened by her. He'd laughed off Janet's bouts of jealousy when he'd mentioned Izzy's name because at that time he'd never thought of her as anything more than a friend. Now it was difficult to think of her as anything other than someone he wanted to share his bed with again.

As he stood there, appreciating the dusting of freckles across her nose and the stunning red hair most women would pay a fortune to try and replicate, she suddenly crumpled to the ground.

'Izzy?' His heart leapt into his mouth and he sprinted towards her, their perfect day shattered at the thought of something happening to her.

She was spread-eagled on the grass, her eyes still closed.

'Izzy?' He dropped to his knees and called her name again, before throwing off his backpack in case his medical skills would be required. Perhaps he had asked too much of her in coming here when she hadn't been herself recently, but he'd wanted to do something for her since it was his fault she felt she couldn't confide in him any more. He was sure it was because she regretted sleeping with him, but he couldn't change what had happened between them, even if he'd wanted to.

He leaned over her, his face close to hers, listening for signs she was still breathing. Her chest continued to rise and fall, and he could feel her soft breath on his cheek.

Suddenly, her eyes snapped open and he was staring into the depths of those sea-green pools. In that moment he was transported back to that night-which-should-not-be-named, when they had been lying in his bed together, naked and wanting. Izzy was looking at him the same way she had then, her eyes and her body asking him to hold her, kiss her, love her. He didn't think he'd be able to resist any more now than he had then, and it was only the impact of those past actions on their relationship that made him pull back. Today was about improving relations between them, not making their working environment more awkward.

'I hope you're happy now you've almost killed me.' Izzy sat up and brushed off any suggestion that she'd ever wanted him to do anything other than feel guilty about bringing her out into the wild.

He sat back on his heels and whistled out a quivering breath. 'Don't ever do that to me again. You nearly gave me a heart attack.'

'Now you know how it feels. I'm not moving again until we've refuelled.' She rolled over onto her side and reached for the food supplies stashed in his bag.

'There are kinder ways to let me know you're hungry than fake fainting, you know!' He pulled out a bottle of water from the side pocket in the rucksack and flicked the condensation from the cold bottle at her, getting them back on the pranking friends track rather than the almost kissing past lovers one on his mind.

She let out a shriek before dissolving into a fit of adorable giggles. It was good to hear her laugh again and for him to do it with her. He realised then it had been a while since he'd found the fun in anything. Izzy in any capacity was good for his soul.

'I'll get you back for that when you least expect it,' she vowed, eyes narrowed as she took a bite of her sandwich.

Cal stretched out on the grass beside her. They did spend the majority of their time in isolated countryside, going to the rescue of those in mortal danger, but there was no time to enjoy the surroundings. It was nice to chill out here in the open and better still with company.

Izzy handed over the parcel of sandwiches she'd made. He'd suggested a pub lunch, but she'd insisted on a picnic. Come to think of it, she'd been doing a lot of that recently, bringing her own lunches, forgoing their usual coffee runs in favour of her ever-present water bottle. He harked back to that day in the café when she'd struggled to scrabble together a few pounds for a tip. The awful realisation of what was going on made it hard for him to swallow his mouthful of food.

'I hate to sound like a broken record but is there something wrong? I'd really hate to think you were suffering and hadn't come to me for help.'

He saw the flicker of anxiety on her face as she gulped at her water, but it didn't give him any pleasure to know he'd been right. That withholding of information illustrated the decline in their friendship over these past months since they'd slept together when before that they'd used to share everything going on in their lives. He'd feared the repercussions of that intimacy so much it was possible he'd created that distance between them. Worried about getting hurt again so quickly after Janet that he'd backed right out of Izzy's life when she'd needed his support most.

'I, er, I'm just having a few money troubles at the minute. The funeral and everything else has left me a bit strapped for cash, but I'll get by. I always do.' She gave him a bright smile before quickly looking away again, but he didn't believe her problems were as straightforward as she was making out.

He was grateful she'd finally confided in him because he'd never considered the financial implications of losing her partner, regardless of the gambling debts he'd apparently accrued before his death. For one thing he would've imagined Gerry had had some sort of life insurance policy in place to ensure she was protected for this kind of eventuality. Then, of course, there were the everyday practicalities of losing a second income. When Janet had moved out he'd had to cover the mortgage and household bills himself.

He might not have been great at providing Izzy with the emotional support she'd needed but this was something practical he could help with.

'There's no point worrying yourself sick or depriving yourself over the sake of a few pounds. I can give you a loan if that would help dig you out of a hole?' He'd be happier to write her a cheque with no desire to see the money returned but she would never entertain the idea. She was already shaking her head at the alternative suggestion.

'That's a very kind offer but you know I couldn't do that. Taking money from friends always gets messy and I've had enough of being in anyone's debt. Thank you but I'll get through this myself.' Izzy wrapped up the leftovers, tucked them back into the bag and got to her feet, discussion over.

Cal wasn't surprised she'd turned him down because she was notoriously as stubborn as hell but so was he. He was sure there was more to the story, more he could do to help her.

They'd often partnered up on social occasions with their significant others and he'd never believed Gerry good enough for his Fizz. Where she had been the fun and friendly half of the two, Gerry had been her complete opposite. Often sullen and reluctant to be drawn into conversation, he was a closed book and hard to like. He'd never known what Izzy had seen in him but respected her enough not to question her judgement.

Izzy was trying to pick up the fractured pieces of her life in order to move on and Cal was going to be there for her every step of the way. It was about time someone was. Now he knew there was a problem he wasn't going to rest until he knew she was going to be okay. He could be every bit as obstinate as Isobel Fitzpatrick when it came to helping a friend.

* * *

'Ten-year-old girl suffering severe burns after falling against a barbecue.' Izzy recapped the few details they'd been given on the emergency call and directed Mac, the pilot and operations manager, to a clear landing site near the address they'd been given.

Although she didn't wish harm on anyone, never mind a child, the distraction of work was good for her. She had let slip more than she'd intended about her problems to Cal but telling him her money woes was preferable to surprising him with the news he was going to be a father. They'd both messed up, and Cal had enough of his own personal issues to deal with. There was no way she was bringing a child into the world expecting to have someone bailing her out at every hint of trouble. That would be asking for more heartache. She loved him for the offer all the same.

His ex didn't know what she'd thrown away. Cal deserved someone who loved him as much as he'd obviously loved Janet. There was nothing he wouldn't have done for her. Including bringing up someone else's baby as his own if she'd been honest with him instead of stringing him along until she'd been sure her other lover did want her after all.

If he hadn't, Izzy suspected she'd still be letting Cal play happy families with a child who wasn't his. He'd been broken by the betrayal, as anyone would've been, and Izzy had been crushed on his behalf because she knew how important family was to him.

Izzy needed a friend right now, someone who could provide some normality for her when her life was falling down around her, but as soon as he found out about the baby she knew that would change. Things would become untenable when he'd lost the family he'd always dreamed of, only to be left with one he hadn't planned. It was bound to cause some resentment or tempt Cal into interfering in some way, directing that focus from Janet's baby onto hers. She wasn't going to fool herself into thinking anyone had her back any more now than they had before. If there was one thing she excelled at it was picking herself up and dusting herself off after being left in the lurch.

Apart from not wanting to hurt him with her news, she also wanted to avoid him becoming over-protective where she was concerned. When he'd discovered Janet was expecting he'd practically dressed her in bubble wrap, afraid to let her lift a finger to keep mum and baby as safe as possible. Janet had been happy to put her feet up and let Cal run around after her but that was exactly what Izzy didn't want.

She intended to carry on as normal for as long as she could. Being pregnant wasn't a disability, millions of women had gone through it time and time again. Besides, she was almost at the three-month mark and out of the danger stage. If Cal had any inkling he wouldn't have suggested a country ramble, never mind let her carry on with the physical side of her job.

Fitness and strength was a huge part of being air ambulance crew and she loved her job. If nothing else, she needed every penny she could put aside before her maternity leave. She didn't want to think about the cost of childcare for the next eighteen years. From now on she was going to take one day at a time. It was the only way she'd get through these next belly-blossoming months without going doolally.

'Earth to Izzy. I asked if you were ready

for this.' Cal's eyes were on her instead of the lush green scenery whizzing past below. The last thing she needed was him getting distracted on this call with her. There was no room for error when every second counted.

''Course. Why wouldn't I be?' She frowned at him, a warning to mind his own business at work. He knew better than to let personal problems encroach on this already too-small space and make it even more claustrophobic. The pile of bills he thought was her only problem was definitely not something that warranted a discussion here. Especially when she was doing her best not to think about the little bundle who was about to throw her life into more chaos.

Cal gave her the thumbs up as they landed, and she considered the matter closed for now when there was a patient needing their help.

They hiked up the street with their gear to the house with the door already lying open.

'Let's hope someone had the foresight to administer first aid.' It was Cal who said it, although Izzy was thinking the same thing. Providing that immediate care in the aftermath of a burn could make all the difference to the long-term damage.

'I'm sure the switchboard operator would've given them instructions on cooling the burn under tepid water.' They didn't know how serious the burns were but with a child involved the stakes were that much higher. Skin grafts, infection and plastic surgery were all possible, depending on the extent of the burns, and not something a parent would want their baby to go through.

'Hello. Air ambulance crew here,' Cal called into the house as they made their entry.

'We're upstairs in the bathroom.' A woman appeared at the top of the stairs and beckoned them up where there was a group of adults crowded around a sobbing child.

'Okay, could we ask everyone to give us a bit of room, please?' The bathroom was cramped enough for them to work in so Izzy needed to clear out those taking up unnecessary space. Eventually the other family members shuffled out until there was only the child and her parents remaining.

'Hi, I'm Doctor Cal. What's your name?' Cal knelt down beside the youngster, who was trembling and crying as she stood in the bath while her father was hosing her down with a shower head.

'This is Suzy,' her father volunteered, and shut off the water so they could assess her injuries.

'I hear there was an accident with a barbecue?' Although Cal took the lead, Izzy was there to back him up and give assistance where it was needed.

Dad nodded. 'The kids were running about, and she tripped and fell into the barbecue. She stuck her hand out to break the fall and I think that's where most of the damage was done.'

Whilst Cal was inspecting the upper-body burns that had left angry red marks across her chest and shoulders, Izzy gently took her hand to assess the extent of the burns.

'Where do you hurt most, Suzy?'

The child lifted her hand up and Izzy could see where it was beginning to blister.

'We're going to give you something to help with the pain, sweetheart. Cal, do you want to take a look at this?'

His brow furrowed too, and it was clear he wasn't any happier than she was at the sight. 'The chest and shoulder burns I would say are only two per cent partial thickness so we can dress those but I'd prefer a specialist to take a look at that hand. In the meantime, can we get a line in for some pain relief?'

One of the bonuses of transporting patients by helicopter was that they could take them directly to the best centre to treat their injury. In this case they could take little Suzy to the burns unit where plastic surgeons would be there to assess her injury and treat her straight away to limit permanent damage.

'Suzy, you're just going to feel a wee scratch in your hand. We need to give you something to help with the pain. Perhaps Dad can just hold you steady for me? Good girl.' Izzy administered the drugs as instructed by Cal, which would hopefully go some way to making the child comfortable again. It was difficult to watch her suffer and Izzy felt for the mother, who was standing nearby, whispering soothing words to comfort her child, though she must've been racked with guilt and anxiety herself.

Izzy understood motherhood wasn't an easy job when so many had failed her in her childhood, but she was looking forward to the challenges ahead. She wanted her child to know its mother would be there come what may and would relish that role of being needed, bringing a sense of security she'd never experienced herself.

'Dad, are you okay to carry her out to the helicopter? Then we're going to take a quick ride to the hospital. Have you ever been on a helicopter, Suzy?' Cal got them organised and on the move whilst Izzy checked in with the control room to update them on their progress and route.

'No, she hasn't, and neither have I.' Suzy's dad gave a nervous laugh.

'There's nothing to worry about. We'll be at the hospital in twenty minutes tops.' Half the time it would've taken an ambulance and it cut out all the transfers between departments. Izzy knew if it was her daughter she'd be only too glad to have Cal and the helicopter at hand to administer treatment. He was a calm, assured presence in the storm and Izzy hoped that remained true for the one he was about to enter with her.

Once they landed, Cal and Izzy worked together to unbuckle their passengers and get them out of the helicopter. They hurried with the stretcher towards the team waiting for the transfer, but the ground was greasy after the earlier downpour of rain and in Izzy's haste she slipped and landed on her back.

'Izzy, are you all right?' Cal hesitated and offered a hand to help her to her feet, but she was winded and a little disorientated.

'Go. Go.' She waved him on, their patient a priority here, but made no move to get up.

Instead, she lay back and rested her hands protectively on her belly. It was early days and she'd hit the ground hard, as indicated by the pain shooting up her spine.

Those darned hedgehogs were back, pricking her eye sockets and trying to make her cry again, as she wondered if she had been taking too many risks after all. If she hadn't been one hundred per cent sure about wanting this baby, the prospect of having harmed it confirmed it was all she wanted. She needed to know it was safe in there, protected from her stupidity and two left feet. At least she was in the best place possible to find out.

She heard a male voice utter an expletive

and looked up to find Cal standing over her. 'You really hurt yourself, huh?'

He bent down and eased her up into a sitting position. That small act of support was enough to tip her emotionally over the edge. One crack in her defences and the dam broke, tears gushing down her face for the first time since Gerry's funeral.

'I'm pregnant, Cal.' She was finally admitting it now in the hope it made this baby real and lessened the possibility of something happening to it.

'Okay. Okay. We'll get you into the emergency room and I'm sure they can arrange an ultrasound for you to make sure baby's all right. How far along are you?' Cal did his best to remain calm, so he didn't freak her out more than she already was. Regardless, that was exactly what he was doing on the inside.

'Three months.'

Perhaps it was the shock of her news, but it took a moment for it all to sink in for Cal. Gerry had died over five months ago so the baby couldn't be his. On the other hand, he and Izzy had slept together more recently.

Say, three months give or take a few days. His heart tried to take a flying leap out of his mouth. This was his baby. He was going to be a father.

There were a few seconds when he thought he was going to pass out from the sheer significance of what she'd told him. It was cruel timing to discover a one-night stand with his work colleague had resulted in an unplanned pregnancy so soon after the drama of his cheating fiancée and a baby that had turned out not to be his.

Not long ago this news would have made his day. He'd been looking forward to fatherhood since his own parents had died, but circumstances had changed. Along with his outlook on life. He was still reeling from Janet's abuse of his trust and he definitely wasn't ready to be thrown into another drama. Especially one as life-changing as fathering a baby.

He was still scarred by having his last family torn away from him and there was no way of telling how that could manifest itself as this pregnancy progressed. The trauma and loss wasn't something he'd get over easily and it was going to be difficult for him to get used to the idea of becoming a father again when Janet had forever tainted that picture of having a happy family.

It was important to remember this wasn't the ideal scenario for Izzy either after losing Gerry. They were going to have to work together to make sure this baby wasn't affected by the personal baggage they were both carrying from their pasts.

'I'm sorry.' As he got staff to help him transfer her to a stretcher and take her inside, she kept apologising, and he knew why. Izzy was such an empathetic person she was more worried about how the pregnancy would affect him than her.

'You have absolutely nothing to apologise for. We both messed up. The timing isn't the greatest, and neither are the circumstances, but the damage has been done.' He thought he saw her flinch at his choice of words, but he preferred to deal in the truth these days. This wasn't exactly a joyous occasion for either of them, rather something they were going to have to learn to live with.

They didn't love each other, and all indications would suggest she'd rather forget the night they'd apparently conceived this baby.

It wasn't the family he'd planned on having but it wasn't one he could pretend wasn't happening either.

Later, as they transferred for the ultrasound it struck Cal how vulnerable Izzy looked. Once he'd got over his initial shock he could see how frightened she was, tears still falling from her red-rimmed eyes and her hands wringing her handkerchief into knots. For once she was the one who needed support rather than being the one who always provided it.

He squeezed her hand as the sonographer applied gel over her stomach to let her know he was there. If she hadn't wanted him with her she would've made it clear a long time ago.

'If this baby is as tough as its mum, it's not going to be bothered by one wee fall.'

His reassurance was rewarded with a crooked smile, but she was gripping his hand like a vice, further indication that she wanted him with her. It was survival instinct that made him want to disengage her hand from his and turn his back on the epic responsibility of becoming a parent after past experiences. They weren't even in a relationship, therefore giving her more reason to walk out the door when a better option came along. In the end it was his loyalty to Izzy that saw him stick around. This was a second chance for him to be a friend to her and give her the support she needed.

She turned her head to watch the screen as the sonographer moved the Doppler over her slightly rounded belly. Cal had been blind to the obvious signs of her pregnancy, which he would've spotted if he didn't spend so much time in his own head, wallowing in the past or trying to keep her at arm's length. The sickness, the unexpected emotional displays, not to mention the recent aversion to alcohol and greasy food, were blatant clues, along with her new curves.

Watching that hazy blob on the screen come to life brought up so many emotions he had to swallow before he started wailing. It should have been such an exciting time, seeing his baby for the first time, but this was the second time he'd been here. The memories of sitting here, holding Janet's hand, were too painful for him to enjoy the moment, even when the heartbeat sounded out around the room to let them know everything was all right. He was relieved, of course, but emotionally he was just kind of numb.

Izzy's sobs let him know she would love this baby enough for the two of them if it came to it. He lifted her hand to his mouth and kissed it, so she knew he wasn't angry at the situation they'd found themselves in and pleased that the baby was going to be okay.

Then he noticed the frown on the sonographer's face and the quick movement of the Doppler further over Izzy's stomach. She hadn't missed it either.

'What's wrong? I thought the baby was okay?' Her eyes were wide with panic and she almost cut off the circulation in his fingers with her grip. Cal's own breath stilled as they waited for a reply.

'You haven't had your twelve-week scan yet?'

Izzy shook her head. 'I didn't get around to organising that yet.'

The sonographer turned the monitor around for them to see, a smile now evening out her wrinkled forehead as the heartbeat rang out loud and clear once more.

'They'll be able to give you a more accurate reading and confirm dates with you, but I do have some news I can share with you.'

'What? What is it?' It was Cal's turn to voice his concern. He hadn't remained detached from this after all as a swell of nausea rose up inside him at the thought the baby was in any sort of jeopardy.

'I was confirming a healthy heartbeat, but I've found more than one. Meet baby number two.' She turned the screen round so they could see the evidence for themselves.

'You mean...twins?' Izzy's mouth fell open in a half laugh, half sob as it was confirmed with a nod.

'Wow.' It was all he could manage in the wake of the bombshell. Two babies at once. A ready-made family neither of them had planned.

He could see the second reality hit home for her too.

'What am I going to do, Cal?' Struggling for money and now with the prospect of having two children to support, she was turning to him for help. She wouldn't have asked unless she was desperate when she was always so single-minded about controlling her own life. It wasn't a plea he would ignore. These babies were as much his responsibility as they were hers. Neither of them had any family around, or had any intention of getting into another relationship anytime soon. It seemed to him there was only one logical solution to their current situation.

'You'll just have to move in with me.'

CHAPTER THREE

'IT WOULDN'T HURT to think about it. At least until you're back on your feet financially.' Cal was sitting in the chair opposite Izzy in the control room back at base with his feet on the desk, waiting for the next call and driving her to distraction in the meantime.

It was impossible for her to relax since he'd first made that ridiculous suggestion she move in with him to help solve her money problems. Of course, she'd eventually shot him down at the hospital, convinced it had been the shock talking after finding out she was expecting twins. The news had affected her so much she'd almost accepted in the heat of the moment.

It would've been easy to say yes and line up a partner to share the bills and parenting responsibilities but shacking up together for the sake of convenience wouldn't have been fair. Especially to her, when it would give her false hope they could pick up where they'd left off that night in his house. He'd made it clear that wasn't going to be an option, regardless of the new complication in their lives. Every time she thought that attraction between them was raising its head, he backed off, and she had to get it out of her head they could be anything more than friends or she'd never move on from that night.

Cal wasn't promising her that they'd live happily ever after together. In fact, he'd yet to acknowledge wanting to take on any sort of parenting role. This sounded more like offering a friend a sofa to kip on when they were down on their luck. She supposed she should be grateful for that much when he could hardly bring himself to touch her, much less declare his undying love for her, since they'd slept together.

'You know as well as I do it's a foolish notion. I'd appreciate it if you didn't bring it up at work where someone could overhear.' With sharp reflexes she shot out her hand to catch the rubber ball he was bouncing off the wall before the repetitive thud gave her a migraine. It was fair to say it didn't take a lot to rile her these days when she was so full of stress and worry.

'Uh…there's no one here. Mac's on his break.' Smartass had an answer for everything when he knew very well she didn't want him bringing this up again regardless of who was around. This wasn't a matter for gossip fodder or outlandish proposals born of a misguided sense of duty. It was her life.

Izzy unclenched her fist and the ball pinged back into shape. As it turned out, it was a pretty good stress reliever. It saved her wringing anyone's neck.

'You know what I mean. We spend half of our lives talking over headsets and I don't want anything accidentally slipping out. My private life is just that and I'll tell people about the pregnancy in my own time. As for moving in together, we're definitely keeping that between us before anyone gets carried away with the idea.' Her included.

He was saying all the right words but since finding out about Gerry's secret life she'd learned to look beyond mere lip service. Cal was the sort of man who would fulfil his obligations no matter what the personal cost was to him, but she didn't want him to feel trapped. Neither did she want someone else promising her the world and getting her hopes up about playing happy families, only to have them cruelly dashed further down the line.

Her reservations seemed justified when he wasn't giving off the same vibes he had when he'd announced Janet's pregnancy. It was understandable he wouldn't be as excited this time around after everything that had happened, but she didn't see that same desire in him to be a father any more. Her babies deserved the very best she could give them and that didn't include a reluctant dad. She knew what it was like to grow up somewhere you weren't completely wanted, and she vowed to do better by her children as a parent. Even if that meant raising them alone.

Cal's offer might be a temporary solution to her problems, but she knew it would be setting them up for future ones.

'I don't see why you're so against the idea.' He withdrew his long limbs from the desk and sat up in the chair, no longer appearing so relaxed.

'We'll start with the fact we've both recently lost the people we loved and neither of us are in the right state of mind to make a life-changing decision like this. Then there's the whole baby issue. You weren't even prepared for one baby, never mind two. Think of the disruption that's going to cause in your life on a practical level. I didn't tell you before now that I'm pregnant because I didn't want you to feel obligated. I'm not expecting anything from you.'

This wasn't about sparing his feelings, it was about keeping things real. She could raise these babies alone because she would make them her whole world. To have two children at once gave her the family she wanted, and it didn't have to include a man.

'Are you done?' He leaned forward, his face and body rigid as he stared her down, and she knew she'd dented his pride. 'Yes, I'm thinking with my head instead of my heart but the whole love thing didn't work out for me. I don't like thinking of you in that flat with goodness knows who knocking on your door in the dead of night. My house is big enough to accommodate everyone and I've already got a nursery. We might have to double up on some things but that's easily arranged. I want to be a good friend to you as well as provide a stable home for you all.'

'What happens when you meet someone else and want to set up a home with them? Where would that leave me? Alone, penniless and out on the street with two children.'

After Gerry she knew she'd find it harder than ever to trust another man get close anyway, but her babies took priority over everything. Not that she'd be a catch, broke, with two children by another man. Cal might believe that he'd never get into another relationship, but he could change his mind over time. He was handsome, smart and too caring for his own good. There was no reason he couldn't have it all if he wanted. A woman would have to be a lunatic to turn him down. Or simply trying to save him from his own sense of chivalry.

'Think about it.' He edged his chair closer to hers and her heart picked up an extra beat.

He hadn't mentioned the babies in his argument but if Izzy was to entertain the idea of moving in she'd need some sort of assurance he was going to be a father to these babies. She couldn't live with him and pretend he was nothing more than a landlord to them. It was one thing being asked to forget what had happened between them but quite another if he thought she'd overlook that. Her children deserved a father who was crazy about them, so enamoured she'd be willing to forget everything she'd gone through in the past and risk it all again for their happiness.

She'd made the mistake of believing she'd finally found a forever home with Gerry, going all in and risking her heart in the hope things would work. The crash hadn't been his fault, but the debts and the gambling had proved he'd never put her first.

She couldn't commit herself to someone else who treated her babies the same way.

'We're friends who made a mistake, Cal, let's leave it at that. I hereby relinquish you from any responsibility.' Weary from the debate going on inside and outside her head about the subject, Izzy decided to put an end to it once and for all.

'I don't think that's your call. It took two of us to make these babies. Is that what's stopping you from letting me be involved? I mean, I wouldn't force you to be a *proper* wife, if you're worried about that?' The tinge of red flushing his complexion told him exactly what part of marriage he was thinking about.

Sleeping with Cal was something she was doing her best to keep from her mind. They had much more domestic matters to discuss, but now he'd mentioned it the image of the two of them rolling around in bed was suddenly on her mind. If they got married and planned a future together then that was something they would probably succumb to again. They both had physical needs and it would be, well, convenient as well as enjoyable. The idea held definite appeal for her, but she couldn't tell him that in case he thought she'd planned the whole thing.

'A *proper* wife? You mean like having dinner waiting on the table for you coming home after work, warming your slippers by the fire and generally losing my identity to keep my man happy? I don't fancy your chances, mate.'

'You know exactly what I mean, Fizz.' The lopsided grin and darkening eyes dared her to think about it again.

Now she was more uncomfortable than

ever because she was imagining Cal as a permanent feature in her bed. A hot man who was offering her a bed and who'd already proved he could make her happy in that department made for an excellent sales pitch.

'Job! RTC. Two vehicles.' That was all Mac had to say to get the crew moving.

Cal jumped in the front of the helicopter with him to direct him to the crash site and waited for Izzy to get into the back.

'Check doors and harnesses.'

'Locked and secured.' Izzy followed his cue with the safety checks and they were in the air within minutes of the emergency call coming into the control room.

'Okay, land paramedics are on the scene and have requested our attendance. Patients are currently being assessed.' It wasn't long before Cal could see the site of the accident for himself as there was such a hive of activity going on around it. The flashing lights of the ambulance and the high-visibility vests of the crews already working to free the passengers were like a beacon signalling the location.

From the air it was easy to see the car that

had taken the brunt of the damage on the passenger side. Although they wouldn't be sure what they were dealing with until they reached the ground.

The fire service on scene seemed to be concentrating their efforts on that particular vehicle as the air ambulance landed in a field nearby and Cal and Izzy went to join them. The other vehicle in the crash had damage to the front but the driver was receiving treatment in the back of the ambulance.

One of the paramedics came to update them on events and as it had appeared from the outset, the girl still trapped in the car, Stephanie, was the one they were most concerned about. He and Izzy followed him over to the patient and while Cal assessed any visible injury, Izzy made strides to comfort the young woman pinned inside the car.

'Hi, I'm Izzy, with the air ambulance. Now, the doctor's just going to take a look at your injuries before we attempt to move you, Stephanie. Okay?'

'Okay.' She didn't sound convinced, but she was conscious and was a point in her favour.

'I want you to take nice deep breaths,

Stephanie.' Cal crouched down to get as close to her as he could. 'Can you tell me where the pain is?'

'My left arm and left leg. They hurt so bad.' She was crying now but it was Cal's job to determine whether that was caused by fear or injury.

'I know they do and we're going to give you some pain relief, but I can't see any blood so we're going to try and get you out of here.' He gave the fire crew the nod to start cutting the roof so they could get better access to her, but they still had to be careful. Although there was no visible bleeding, there was a chance she could be bleeding internally, and she had most likely broken her arm and leg.

'There's going to be a lot of noise and vibration while the crew work on cutting the roof of the car, Stephanie.' Izzy reached in and held her hand until the roof finally came off.

'Good girl. You're doing really well. I know it hurts, but we need to get you to the helicopter.' Izzy kept her vigil at Stephanie's side, reassuring her she would be all right and providing some comfort to the frightened girl. It struck him more in that moment than ever what a great mum she was going to make. Her compassion and nurturing side was everything a kid could want in its mother. He should know. He had his own parents to hold up as a shining example of how family life should be. It was a shame he apparently hadn't carried on that legacy when he was avoiding the subject of becoming a dad himself.

'I need some help here to get her onto the stretcher.' He concentrated on the job he was good at, administering some strong pain relief to the patient before they attempted extrication, and called the other paramedics and fire crew to assist with the transfer. 'Ready. Brace. Roll.'

They worked together to get her onto the stretcher, causing as little pain as possible in the circumstances. Izzy put a splint on Stephanie's injured arm and they put a pelvic binder around her to protect against any internal bleeding. Once she was stabilised as best they could manage, Cal again asked for assistance in carrying her over to the ambulance.

'Ready. Brace. Go.' They moved in synch,

ensuring they didn't jolt her about too much, and Izzy radioed in a progress report and an ETA of their arrival at the nearest hospital.

When it came to work, and life-or-death situations, Izzy's confidence and decisiveness were exactly what was needed. In her personal life, however, that assertiveness that she could do everything on her own was ticking him off. He mightn't be the daddy-to-be she wanted for her children, but he wasn't Gerry either. Izzy should know him better than believing he'd walk away from this pregnancy because it was inconvenient. He had no intention of leaving her to pick up the pieces alone. As long as she dropped those defences enough to see the idea to move in was for her benefit, not his.

Janet had broken everything important in him beyond repair—his trust, his belief that he could replicate the happy family he'd grown up in, and, crucially, that urge in him to be a father at all. Still, she hadn't managed to take away the basic desire to be a decent human being. The mother of his future children was in trouble and he was going to do right by her.

If being broke, alone and pregnant with

twins had been an illness, Izzy wouldn't have thought twice about finding a cure. Cal knew he wasn't perfect but as far as he could see he was the best option she had, and he would do his best to make her see that. They were in this together whether they liked it or not.

It was getting harder for Izzy to switch off after a shift. Stephanie was young, and she would heal with time, but that initial phone call to let Stephanie's parents know what had happened had been painful. She'd asked Izzy to make the call for her and to play down her injuries, but her mother's fear had been almost palpable. Izzy wasn't a parent yet, but this pregnancy was already changing her in ways she hadn't prepared for and she knew once the babies were here their safety would be the only thing that mattered to her. There were only six months before they arrived, and she had nothing in place for them except uncertainty.

To his credit, Cal hadn't pushed her any more on moving in with him and had been willing to talk over her concerns regarding their patient's prognosis in a debriefing ses-

overwhelmed Izzy with the fuzzy warmth of a love she'd forgotten existed. Helen was her bestie, a sister and a mother all wrapped in one. If it hadn't been for her, Izzy wouldn't have known love existed at all. She was the one good thing Izzy had had in her childhood and the only connection from that time she didn't want to lose. They'd kept in touch, but text messages and video calls weren't the same as a much-needed hug.

'And who's this?' Cal asked, peering into the pram where the baby was grizzling.

'This is Oliver and it's nearly time for his dinner.' Helen lifted him out of the pram as he made his impatience known at having to wait another second for his next feed.

'Feel free to feed him in here. We'll make sure everyone gives you some privacy.'

'I hope I'm not putting you out, Iz, by turning up here unannounced? I just wanted to see you.' Helen slung the changing bag over her shoulder and manoeuvred baby and pram out the door Cal was holding open.

'Not at all. I'm glad you came. Our shift's over so give us a minute to get changed out of our gear then we can go somewhere for a catch-up.'

sion on the ride back from the handover at the hospital, leaving her free from any additional worries to keep her awake at night.

'Your usual?' Cal rested his hand on her back the second they made it back to base.

She nodded, having become accustomed to their sober chats. It wasn't as though they'd been in the habit of rolling home steaming drunk, but the nature of their relationship had changed along with their drinking habits. They'd become more than mates when she'd gone to him about the double life she'd discovered Gerry had been leading and now they had a connection that went beyond an emotional level.

Regardless of her vow to do everything single-handedly when that little blue line had appeared on the pregnancy test, Cal had made her realise how much she needed that level of support. His company alone reminded her she wasn't alone, even if she didn't intend forcing him to do it on a permanent basis.

'Tea and a chat is exactly what I need right now,' she said as she pushed open the office door.

'Good because that's exactly why I'm

here.' It took a few seconds for the sight of the blonde woman standing in the room to register with Izzy, and when it did she flung herself at her childhood friend.

'Helen? What on earth are you doing here?' she managed to sob out in the midst of the bear hug.

'Your friend Calum here persuaded me to pay a visit and clearly he was right. You're not yourself. What on earth is wrong, Iz? I've never seen you like this.' Helen prised her off to take a good look at her.

Izzy glanced at a sheepish Cal. 'But how…?'

'I thought you might need a friend.'

She did but she hadn't realised he'd been taking notes when she'd mentioned Helen, never mind take the time out to track her down. He'd obviously been concerned on more than a practical level about her welfare. Simply finding out he knew that much about her life and cared enough to make that contact instantly perked up her mood. Although he hadn't been gushing about becoming a father, his actions showed he was thinking very deeply about how this was affecting her. She hoped that was a sign he'd eventually

warm to the idea of being a father be superficial level, but he clearly hadn't their most important news.

'Thank you, Cal.' Izzy gave him a peck on the cheek to show her apprecia for his thoughtfulness and counted her lucky to have these two special people in life. Her babies deserved to have the sam

'I'm so happy to see you.' Izzy turn her attention back to Helen in case effusiv thanks made Cal think twice about makin such gestures in the future.

'I didn't come on my own.' Helen stepped aside to reveal a gorgeous pram with an even more gorgeous bundle wrapped inside.

'Oh, my goodness, you brought him with you?' Helen had given birth six months ago, just before Gerry's accident, but with everything going on she hadn't been able to find time to go and visit the new arrival. There was also a part of her afraid to see first-hand the trials she'd yet to face as a new mum.

'We thought we'd have a day out on the train to see Auntie Isobel and let Daddy catch up on some sleep.'

The thought that her friend had trekked the whole way here with a baby to surprise her

'Will you be joining us, Calum?' As subtle as ever, Helen extended the invitation, no doubt in the hope she could pair him off with Izzy. Since she'd become a happy married she'd expected Izzy to join the club with her. Perhaps it was Helen's blissful experience of marriage that had convinced Izzy to stick it out with Gerry and hope they could eventually achieve the same idyll. Izzy hadn't told her about the pregnancy but that would likely fuel her search for a hubby for her and she certainly didn't need any more encouragement where Cal Armstrong was concerned.

'Um…'

'Of course he will. You haven't got anything else to do have you, Cal?' She knew he didn't and it was important he get used to being part of her personal life. Biology had dictated he was included in this family of hers, but she was going to make sure he was connected to these babies by more than duty to do the right thing. Love was a staple of a happy childhood and, as she knew too well, life was miserable without it. She wasn't prepared to enter into any sort of arrangement without a guarantee he was in for the long haul.

With Cal along for their coffee date she'd also be less likely to find herself telling Helen about his offer. The last thing she needed was someone egging her on to do something as outrageous as moving in with the reluctant father to her unborn children.

'Actually, I do. That's why I brought Helen here,' he answered with a scowl, dashing any hope he could be cajoled into being part of her life, or their children's.

It was typical that as soon as they got settled with coffee and cake, baby Oliver woke up from his afternoon nap. Helen was trying to soothe him with one hand pushing the pram up and down whilst trying to inject herself with caffeine with the other. However, Oliver's wails continued to disrupt the other customers.

'Can I lift him out so you can finish your coffee in peace?' Izzy was itching to get her hands on the chubby-cheeked cherub for some cuddles. She couldn't wait for the time when she could do this any time she pleased.

'Go for it.' Helen seemed glad to have an extra pair of hands so she could have a break, and Izzy knew when she had two babies to take care of she'd have her work cut out for her. But she didn't care. Her life would finally have purpose and meaning, not to mention love.

Izzy scooped the wriggling bundle out from under his blanket cocoon and the screaming ceased once he was in the cradle of her arms.

'You just wanted to see what was going on, didn't you?' She was lost in those big blue eyes as he stared up at her, putting his trust in her to take care of him.

'Okay, now spill.' It took Helen a nano-second to make it clear she knew there was something going on with her.

'I think someone might need a nappy change.' Izzy held Oliver out as a buffer, preventing his mother from probing for the truth.

'I changed him before we came here, so stop stalling and start talking.' Helen swatted away the feeble attempt to divert her attention.

'Huh?'

'Are you and Cal…you know?' Helen's eyes were bright with bubbling excitement at the prospect of uncovering a new romance.

'I wouldn't blame you. He's gorgeous and he was worried enough about you to phone me. It's obvious he cares about you a lot.'

'What? No. It's only been a few months since I lost Gerry.' She had to remind herself of that too since the memories of her time with him had got lost amongst recent revelations.

'You and Gerry were over a long time before he died, even if you didn't see it then. He was never going to be the man you needed.'

If Izzy had gone to Helen first when she'd discovered Gerry's betrayal she would never have found herself in this mess. It was only when things between her and Cal had subsequently become strained she'd turned to her friend about her troubles, omitting to tell her about Cal's role in her grief counselling. However, that visceral reaction to the circumstances Gerry had left her in, where she'd cursed him up and down, was ammunition Helen was sure to use against her should she believe Izzy was using his death as an excuse not to date again.

'I know there's something going on between you and Calum. I saw the looks you kept giving each other too. As though you were afraid one of you would slip up and say something you shouldn't.'

It was uncanny how well Helen still knew her, even though they only managed a meet up once or twice a year now. Unless she avoided all future contact with Helen she wasn't going to be able to keep the secret much longer. Especially when her bump had to accommodate two surprise bundles.

She put Oliver back in his pram and knocked back the remainder of her decaf coffee, wishing it was a shot of tequila or even an espresso to give her a jolt of bravado. 'I'm pregnant. With twins.'

The words burst out of her mouth before she could stop them, the pressure of keeping the secret to herself too great to hold back. The bombshell was accompanied by the appropriate sound of a crash as Helen dropped her cup on the table.

'Why have you waited this long to tell me?' She mopped up the spilled coffee with a paper napkin, never taking her eyes off Izzy.

'I'm still trying to come to terms with it myself.'

Helen was staring at her, her mouth open about a foot wide. 'Are they—?'

'Yes, they're Cal's. Do you remember I told you about that man who came looking for Gerry? Well, I went to Cal's that night because I knew I'd feel safe there and one thing led to another...' Izzy felt the need to justify what had happened because it seemed so quick after Gerry's death. Although Helen would never have judged her.

'It's no wonder you turned to him after everything you'd been going through. You don't have to explain yourself and Cal seems like a nice guy. I'm sure he'll stand by you.'

'I'm sure he will but that's not enough for my babies. You know what my childhood was like and I want more for these two. Cal is still hesitant about the whole parenting thing and I'd rather go it alone than have him only as a financial backer.'

'Well, if anyone's strong enough to do this on their own it's you, Iz. Wow. I can't believe you're really pregnant.' Helen reached across the table to give her a hug.

'Neither can I. It's a scary prospect.'

'I take it you're, what, two or three months gone? What are the plans?' She was vastly over-estimating Izzy's ability to process the situation and come up with a solution.

'I…er…haven't actually known for that long.'

'Have you told work?'

'Not yet.'

'Booked into prenatal classes?'

'Not yet.'

'Isobel… Have you even started taking your folic acid supplements?'

'I've been busy.'

It wasn't much of an excuse when she had no life outside work any more, but Izzy's way of dealing with her shock pregnancy had been not dealing with it.

'You're going to have to get organised,' Helen scolded, and immediately started scribbling a list of things for her to do in her personal organiser.

'You know I'm bad at this kind of thing.' She wasn't the type who pinned to-do lists to her fridge, or even marked appointments on a calendar. No, Izzy was more a spur-of-the-moment kind of girl who was used to thinking only about herself and doing what suited her.

'Well, you're going to have to get good at it pretty damn quick.' Serious-Helen face stared at her across the table until Izzy hung her head in shame.

'I know, but where the hell do I start?' She was so overwhelmed by the sheer magnitude of tasks and appointments that she'd avoided dealing with anything so far.

'Start with this.' Helen ripped out the page from her planner and slid it across the table. 'Your midwife will help you devise a birth plan. You *do* have a midwife?'

'Of course.'

'Good. What about after the birth? Have you given any thought to childcare?'

If Izzy had had a proper mother, she imagined she'd have received the same grilling as her friend was giving her now. A parent who cared might have been able to help her out with childcare and hold her hand during the pregnancy. Given a chance, Helen would do the same but she lived too far away and had a family of her own to look after.

'Cal asked me to move in with him. I said no. We're just friends. That night should never have happened.'

'It's sweet that Calum wants to take care of you. If you had better taste in men you'd have snatched him up a long time ago.'

'Yes, well, I'm done trusting men. I want to do this on my own.' She didn't, not really, but it seemed to her it was the only way to protect herself and the babies from unnecessary suffering.

'Clearly you trust him, or you wouldn't have turned to him for help in the first place.'

'I trust him in *that* way, it's just…' It was difficult to put it into words when she wasn't entirely sure why his interference frightened her so much.

'You're worried he'll hurt you the same way Gerry did?'

'Yes. No. I don't know.' He could only cause her that level of pain if she saw him as more than a friend and that wasn't what he was necessarily offering. Although there had been that nod towards a physical relationship, which had shaken her to the core, but she wasn't sharing that with Helen. The reason she was holding back was because she was afraid she'd get in too deep when she had even more to lose if it all fell apart.

'There's nothing to say you have to make a commitment beyond the rent to enjoy the benefits of what he's offering.'

Izzy's mind leapt to those images of them

exploring each other's bodies again, but she decided to play the innocent. 'What do you mean?'

'You could do the fun stuff that goes with being a couple without the headaches. A housemates with benefits deal. If it doesn't work out you both move on without any baggage.'

'Wouldn't it seem as though I was using Cal by doing that? Besides, he hasn't shown any interest in me in *that* way since I spent the night with him.' It sounded feasible in theory, but Izzy was worried that was only because she was becoming desperate.

Helen shrugged. 'He offered, didn't he, with no strings? Trust me, I've seen the way he looks at you and I can read between the lines…'

This outside perspective on their situation no longer made Cal's suggestion as ludicrous as she'd first thought. They might be able to make this work after all.

CHAPTER FOUR

'CAN I GIVE you a lift home?' Cal didn't want to walk away and leave Izzy at the train station alone. She'd been very quiet since they'd waved Helen and Oliver off. Although the afternoon was supposed to help lift her spirits, he suspected it had been a huge dose of reality for her, seeing her friend struggle to look after the baby on her own for the afternoon. Not that she'd struggled per se, but it was very different trying to have a coffee and a quiet chat when you had a baby in tow. Something Izzy was going to have to get used to if she kept refusing all offers of help.

'Sure.' She barely glanced his way as she led the way to the car, deep in thought about something he wasn't privy to.

They buckled up in continued silence and Cal was afraid she was going to retreat back into her world alone. Izzy had been let down once too often and he wasn't going to add himself to that list by shirking his responsibilities.

'Helen seems lovely.'

'She is,' Izzy confirmed, her gaze fixed firmly on the road ahead. She was remarkably sullen compared to how buoyant she'd been in her friend's company and Cal knew it was probably because he'd refused to be dragged along with them. It was one thing offering her a lifeline but quite another getting involved in her personal life.

Left to his own devices, he'd batten down the hatches at home and prevent another woman from setting foot in his inner sanctum in case she broke his heart too, but these were exceptional circumstances. Given Izzy's reluctance, he knew she was every bit as wary about moving in together as he was, but they had to set their own comfort aside in favour of the babies. What they needed more than anything was a stable home environment.

'Olly's adorable too.' The baby had been a reminder of his sisters and their offspring, who were scattered across the UK now there was nowhere for them to congregate with the family home gone. He missed being an uncle. He missed being anything to anyone.

He started the engine, resigned to the fact that Izzy was never going to agree to anything unless he fully committed to parenthood. Something he wasn't ready to do and he wasn't going to make false promises.

Then she turned to him and said, 'Take me home with you, Cal.'

If she'd been any other woman and he any other man, that sentence could've been construed as a precursor to another night of passion. There was a part of him that still held a spark of hope that that was her intention, but he knew Izzy better than that. This was a sign of something other than a sudden overwhelming urge to bed him again.

He derailed the inappropriate train of thought, wondering if it was a sign he might not be able to take a vow of celibacy where Izzy was concerned after all.

'Any, um, particular reason?' He did his best to keep his voice neutral, so she didn't guess where his mind had gone to.

'If I'm going to consider your proposal seriously, I'd like to see the goods on offer.

I mean, your assets…the house…you know what I mean.' Her flustering combined with her heightened colour made him think he hadn't been alone in his less-than-pure thoughts.

He resisted the obvious teasing when they were beginning to make a breakthrough. This was the first hint he'd given that she was taking his suggestion seriously, so he didn't want to scare her off by turning it into something sordid. Whatever scenario his neglected libido had been conjuring up would have to give way to more important issues.

Cal had never been the type of guy to choose one-night stands over a meaningful relationship, but this wasn't about him. Sex wasn't something he expected in return for anything but if it was something they both decided they wanted as part of the deal, he wasn't going to say no.

Although he was still wondering what had brought her round to his initial way of thinking.

'Does this sudden turnaround have something to do with Helen?' He'd be surprised if Izzy had confided in her about his idea and even more so if her friend had advised her to proceed with it. From the outside it would've sounded absurd even to him, and he got the impression Helen was protective of Izzy and probably the closest thing to family she had. Apart from him of course. If their roles had been reversed he'd have been suspicious of him and his motives too. Still, if he'd won over her friend then he wasn't going to complain. Izzy would know Helen only had her best interests at heart, even if she doubted him.

'I told her about the babies.'

'Oh, okay. How did that go down?'

Izzy smiled for the first time since they'd been alone again. 'She's over the moon and insisted on writing me a pregnancy to-do list. It felt good, though, telling someone. Other than you, I mean. It's like I'm allowed to get excited about this now.'

She rested her hand on her belly, looking more at ease with the pregnancy than he'd seen so far.

'So you should. It's a special time.' Just not especially to him when it was a reminder of all the mistakes he'd made when it came to relationships.

'I suppose we could be housemates, landlord and tenant, whatever you want to call it, but I will be contributing to the household bills.'

'If that's what you want.' It stung a little that she wasn't interested in something more, but he'd take it.

'That's what I want. At least, I think it is.'

'I know, you still want to take a peek at the goods. I guess you can't have too much of a good thing after all.' He was rewarded with a playful nudge for his teasing.

He'd wasted time in a relationship with Janet when he could've been raising a family with someone who'd wanted to be with him. The whole idea of parenting to him had entailed being an active participant. From changing nappies and doing night feeds right through to playing football or driving to dance recitals, he'd been willing to do it all. Now, though, he could see the merits of being one of those back-seat dads. Izzy didn't really want to be with him either so getting attached seemed a pointless exercise, but he could offer these children a home. For however long it was needed.

He and Izzy weren't star-crossed lovers, but they had their feet on the ground and a more realistic view of life now they'd found out the hard way that love couldn't solve everything.

'I want to get a feel for the place and see if I can picture us all living there together.'

They'd be a modern family of convenience created by circumstance and friendship if not in the conventional sense.

Once Izzy saw the nursery and the potential space to raise her children he knew she'd agree to move in. His house would finally become a home. Just for someone other than him.

It wasn't that Izzy had never seen Cal's place before, they often called at each other's houses and sometimes shared a takeaway, but she'd never taken much notice of the surroundings. This time she wanted to see it from a different perspective. She was viewing his house with the prospect of moving in. With him. And their babies. Possibly for ever. Well, it had to be preferable to spending the rest of her days in that poky flat at the top of a flight of stairs, which she could barely afford. If she'd ever pictured this scenario she might have chosen somewhere with access for a twin pram.

Although that would have demanded an even larger chunk of her wages to cover costs. She had to face it, no matter what decision she might have made, the minute she'd thrown in her lot with Gerry, she'd been in trouble.

It was probably a blessing that Cal had thrown her a lifeline and an opportunity to raise their children in a proper home. One she knew would be a supportive environment, even though they wouldn't be together as a couple.

As they pulled up outside the house she was already seeing the possibilities it offered in comparison to her own home. She got that fluttering in her chest as she imagined the green lawn littered with children's toys and opportunities for the babies to play outside. A garden wasn't something she'd had on her wish list when house hunting before, but now she could see how perfect it would be for family life. The detached house surrounded by trees and shrubbery with a driveway secured with high gates made it private and secure.

The size of the house, the grounds and the location made it a highly prized property but for a mother-to-be it was the scope for safe play and adventure that made it valuable. If she did a side-by-side comparison with the square of parched communal land littered with oddments of her neighbours' patio furniture Cal would have sold the whole idea to her based solely on the garden.

'Are you okay?' It was only when he spoke she realised he'd already cut the engine and had no idea how long they'd been sitting in silence whilst she plotted her imaginary playground. It explained why he suddenly sounded nervous about having her here when she hadn't showed him any sign she was happy about it.

'Yes. Sorry. I was miles away. You said something about a nursery?' She unclipped her seatbelt, keen to do her virtual interior decorating too.

Cal didn't waste any time opening up the house, probably worried she'd change her mind again. 'Obviously we'd furnished it for the babies, so you can use anything in there or you're free to put your own stamp on things.'

He led her up the stairs and she remembered the last time she'd followed him to his room at the end of the hall. That had been the moment everything had changed.

'So, er, this is the nursery,' he said, opening the door to a bright, beautiful room that took Izzy's breath away.

'Cal, it's gorgeous and bigger than my flat.' Which meant there was sufficient space for another cot to match the beautiful white cradle already there.

The white room highlighted with silver-star details mapped out an amazing bright galaxy on the walls and made a neutral space to suit any taste or gender. There were accents of pastel pinks, blues and yellows in the furnishings to break up the dazzling white, and the thick silver carpet underfoot was luxuriously expensive. Everything from the pretty star-embroidered blankets to the pine rocking chair in the corner festooned with plump cushions was tailored for comfort as well as appearance.

'I'm sure you'll want to change a few things to suit your own taste so let me know what you have in mind and I'll get on it.'

'Did you have an interior designer in to do

this?' It looked as though someone had copied a page out of a magazine, everything was so perfectly matched and positioned.

Cal picked up a soft fuzzy sheep from a stack of toys on the dresser and laid it in the crib. 'No, it's all my own work.'

Izzy took another look around and could see how much love and care had gone into making this room baby heaven. He'd been so buoyant in those early months, planning for the baby he'd thought he was going to have with Janet, and she could picture him painstakingly painting every inch of this room in preparation for its arrival.

'I should've known something was wrong when Janet was happy to let me do this alone, without her input. I thought she was simply having a hard time accepting the pregnancy. How stupid was I?' The bitter laugh he gave was directly at odds with the caring man who'd put his heart and soul into creating this loving tribute to a baby who'd never been his.

'You weren't stupid. You trusted her, you were in love with her, and she betrayed you in the worst possible way. None of it was your fault.' She rested her hand on his shoulder to show him she was on his side. Who wouldn't be when a man this endearing had been left heartbroken and bereft, essentially grieving for a baby who'd never come home with him?

'Thanks.' When he covered her hand with his, his warmth enveloping her, she knew he was grasping for that connection he'd lost with Janet. An uneasy sense that there was more behind his motives to have her here other than being a good friend began to slither beneath her skin.

'Cal, you didn't ask me to move in just to fill the space Janet left behind, did you?' The one that had a baby-shaped void right next to it.

No amount of saving on her bills would convince her that this was a good idea if that was the reason, because she would never be a replacement for the fiancée he'd lost, and her babies weren't up for negotiation.

'Of course not.' He turned his head so violently to shoot down that theory that he jerked her hand away. 'I told you, you can do whatever you want in here. It's not some sort of shrine. I just thought it was a shame to let all of this go to waste.'

His defensive attitude suggested there might be more behind his reasons than he even realised. As long as she remembered the history here and didn't get sucked into playing the role recently vacated by his ex, they could hopefully cohabit without anyone reading something into the arrangement that wasn't there.

'It would be when I'm going to need two of everything. We could keep the furniture and redecorate, I suppose. It's beautiful, but I do think it might be better all round for something fresh. If you're on board with that?' It was a compromise intended to make things less weird.

'Does that mean you're moving in?' The Cal she recognised immediately wrapped her in a hug and Izzy let herself revel in that moment of intimacy. He was the only person who provided her with that sense of security she found in the circle of his arms.

To have someone who could do that for her on a regular basis, and she was going to need lots of hugs for the foreseeable future, was a definite point in Cal's favour. They were friends and soon to be housemates, with no one else close enough to provide this strength they seemed to find in each other.

She was certain that tingling sensation that travelled from her head to her toes and all the extremities in between when he touched her or held her was merely residual memory of their last, more intimate contact. It was tempting to burrow into his chest like a little dormouse seeking shelter for the winter, but she managed to keep herself in check and dragged herself out of his embrace before she got too used to using him as a crutch. She had to do this on her own. Cal was her back-up. Someone to give her a boot up the backside when she needed it, just as she'd done for him.

As soon as she stepped out of his personal space the sudden sense of loss slipped out of her mouth on a sigh. 'I'll need to see the bedroom before I make a final decision.'

The corners of his mouth tilted up as he deliberately misinterpreted her comment. It hadn't escaped her notice either that he hadn't attempted to end the too-long hug. Their previous conversation about exploring all aspects of marriage sprang to mind again and her pulse rocketed. Perhaps she should avoid all *double entendres* for the sake of her blood pressure from now on.

'*My* bedroom. The room where I'll be sleeping. Alone.' The emphasis was as much for herself as Cal when it would be far too convenient to jump into bed together should the mood strike them. That sort of blurry line would make things messy when they had to work and live together. Essentially that would put them in a relationship neither of them wanted. This new set-up was supposed to avoid the emotional uncertainty that came as part of a couple package.

'Spoilsport.' The wink he gave her sent shivers through her as though he'd danced his fingers along her spine and she followed him like a devoted puppy into another bright and spacious room.

'You really should think about a sideline as an interior decorator,' she said, taking in her proposed new accommodation. It had a modern appearance but with a lovely homely feeling.

'I'll give it some consideration when I get too old and decrepit for jumping out of helicopters.' He deflected the compliment with another self-deprecating comment, but Izzy couldn't imagine him as anything other than in his prime at any age.

'You'll certainly save me a job, anyway. I won't have to redecorate or attempt to dismantle my flat-pack furniture to move in here. I assume fixtures and fittings are included?'

'Everything I have is at your disposal.' His exaggerated bow gave him the air of a handsome prince giving her the keys to his kingdom, which she liked to think included a secret library somewhere.

'In that case, I can cancel the removal van. Everything I want is right here.' She was referring to the solid pine furniture the entire contents of her flat could fit into but found herself staring at Cal instead.

'What about the bed? No one's ever used the one in here, but you might prefer to have your own.' He walked past her to sit on the end of the mattress, bouncing up and down to show her the obvious quality of the springs.

The lumpy, barely held together with chipboard thing she called a bed, which was also half the size of this sleep playground, couldn't compete.

'Are you kidding? I could live in this.' She threw herself on top of the bed so she was flat out, staring at the ceiling. Her bouncing knocked Cal off balance until he ended up lying beside her, only a hair's breadth away.

'I'm glad you're moving in.'

'I haven't agreed yet.' She was still clinging on to that one last thread of control.

'What else can I do to convince you?' Cal's husky voice was almost enough to persuade her to do anything.

That was it. The final tie to her logical brain pinged free and left her to the mercy of her hormones. They were lying so close to one another there was nowhere else to look but at his eyes, his lips... He was staring at her mouth too, clearly thinking the same thing—how nice a kiss would be right now. Breathtakingly slowly they were gravitating towards each other, closing those last few millimetres separating them from heaven, and insanity.

Izzy sat up, breaking the thrall of his hypnotic gaze. 'I think we should get one thing straight from the beginning, Cal. I want to move in and I appreciate everything you're doing for me, but I think we should take the, er, physical side of this relationship off the cards.'

With that bombshell Cal sat up too so they were both perched uncomfortably on the end of the bed. 'Certainly. I wouldn't dream of using this arrangement to take advantage of you. We'll keep things strictly platonic.'

The longer she spent in his company the more she'd anticipate spending nights in bed with him, but she knew the novelty of having her around would wear off as it always did.

'I think it's for the best.'

'So, we're free to date other people if and when we're ready for that?'

Izzy didn't know why that question shook her when he was a hot-blooded male, not a monk. She supposed it was because she couldn't imagine getting involved in another relationship and had thought he was of the same opinion. It wasn't fair to expect him to remain celibate for ever because she'd prefer it, but the thought of him bringing other women home with him was painful. Ridiculous, when she'd been the one drawing the line in the sand and deeming her side a sex-free zone.

She knew the one flaw in this plan could

be if she feil for Cal, confusing his sense of duty for something more. Something that could only ever end badly.

CHAPTER FIVE

'YOU SHOULD BE sitting with your feet up.' Cal marked out the light switch with masking tape so it didn't get splattered with paint and made sure the dust sheet was covering the whole floor.

'Why? You're not and unless I'm mistaken we've had exactly the same workload today.' Displaying her usual obstinacy, Izzy refused to take it easy after another hectic shift.

'Yes, but I'm not carrying two extra loads with me.' He pointed his paintbrush at her belly, which was noticeably more rounded in her form-fitting grey jersey top and black leggings.

'You promised you wouldn't mollycoddle me,' she reminded him, and began rolling on the pale turquoise paint she'd chosen to cover the nursery walls.

'There's a difference between mollycoddling and doing you a favour. I'm happy to do all the grunt work here.' That way he could make sure she had some down time. So far, since moving in with him, she hadn't shown any signs of slowing down. He had managed to convince her to let him carry the few belongings she had with her but only after an exhaustive debate. Eventually she'd accepted he was merely trying to be a gentleman and not treating her as an invalid. Despite his reservations about his suitability as a parent to these babies, he was doing his best to ensure they'd want for nothing, and that included a strong, healthy mother.

'I wouldn't call painting a wall particularly taxing.' Izzy proved her point by covering most of the mid-section in just a few strokes.

'The fumes can't be good for you.' He simply wanted her to take care of herself if she wouldn't let him do it for her.

It had been a huge part of Janet's pregnancy for him, fussing around and feeling useful in some capacity when he hadn't been able to help with any of the physical toll pregnancy had taken on her.

Seeing how active and reluctant Izzy was

to let her condition become an excuse to slow down made him wonder if Janet had been laughing behind his back the whole time he'd been skivvying for her. Of course she had, the baby wasn't his and while he'd been preparing to become a father she'd been planning to leave him.

Izzy wouldn't take advantage of him in that way when he'd had to work so hard to get her this far.

Despite referencing the possibility of entering into a physical relationship, he knew it would never stay solely in the bedroom and he didn't want to jeopardise what they had here. It was simply a reaction to the attraction that had sprung to life rather quickly after their respective heartaches. Besides, apart from the scars they still bore from those ill-fated relationships, they'd be too tired dealing with two small children to think about dating or anything else.

'I promise if I start to feel faint or sick I'll hang up my paint roller.' It was a concession he was willing to accept when she didn't often make them.

'Good. No stretching either. I'll get the ladder and do the top bits.' There was no need for her to overdo things when he was there to pick up the slack.

'I assume I'm allowed to do the bottom bits? I can sit on the floor to do that. You know, take it easy.' She was making fun of him, but it was better than bristling at him each time he attempted to do something nice for her.

'As long as you don't get under my feet.' She'd already worked her way over to the section he was covering so he let a blob of paint plop onto her head.

'For your sake I hope you didn't do that on purpose.' Izzy lifted her head to look at him, eyes narrowed and lips twitching.

'You know me better than that, Fizz.' He'd never been able to resist riling that temper of hers, such was their dynamic, and he was glad that spark was still there after all this time.

'Hmm.' She knew him too well and he laughed at the apparent scepticism.

Cal resumed painting his part of the wall, only realising he was in serious trouble when he saw her roller paint over the palms of her hands instead of the plasterwork. The next thing he knew those same hands were resting on his buttocks and with one squeeze he knew she'd wreaked her revenge.

'You haven't…' He tried to twist his torso around to see the evidence but the glee on Izzy's face was proof enough that she'd left two turquoise handprints on the backside of his trousers.

'You deserved it.' She was grinning up at him, her eyes full of mischief, challenging him to do something about it.

'Isobel Fitzpatrick, you are in so much trouble…'

She let out a shriek as he dropped his paintbrush and tried to wrestle the roller out of her hands, but Izzy was too quick for him. With sleight of hand she hid her weapon behind her back, forcing him to reach around her to try and get it. Her laugh at his ear made him aware of how close their bodies were, and with the slightest turn of his head his lips were dangerously close to Izzy's.

He heard the hitch in her breath as she realised it too and he wanted so badly to kiss her it took all of his physical strength to back off before he did something stupid. The chemistry was there all right, but Izzy had made it clear she didn't want to repeat past mistakes. Instead he took a sidestep away and carried on decorating as though nothing out of the ordinary had transpired.

'It's just as well these are old clothes, or we'd have people talking about us.' As if. The only people they saw were their colleagues, and the crew had hardly batted an eyelid when they'd told them they were moving in together before they'd explained it was only as housemates. Mac, when Cal had tackled him about the lack of surprise, had explained they'd all thought the two of them had been at it like rabbits for years, despite having had partners for most of that time. Cal put him straight and asked him to pass on the information. The purpose, other than saving Izzy's reputation, was his own pride. He refused to let anyone believe he'd cheated on Janet and deserved what she'd done to him in any way.

It was a conversation he hadn't relayed to Izzy for fear of upsetting her. If he was annoyed there was any suggestion he'd played away on his treacherous ex, he could only imagine the effect it would have on her. The last thing Izzy needed stressing her out was malicious gossip that she'd somehow failed Gerry.

Cal had been blaming himself for months over what had happened between him and Janet, agonising over every disagreement that could have caused her to cheat on him. Izzy might have gone through something similar, wondering what she could've done to prevent the crash from happening, and she didn't need anything more to beat herself up over. Cal would rather put a smile on her face at his expense than give her cause to feel guilty about something she'd never had the power to control. It had taken all this time for him to learn that lesson.

It was only when Izzy had agreed to move in with him that he'd stopped blaming himself for Janet leaving. In some way he'd taken it as confirmation he wasn't as bad a person as he'd begun to believe, that he must've had some redeeming qualities if she was willing to live with him at this crucial time.

'I'll just tell them you're the father of my unborn babies and I'm marking my territory,' she said, following his lead in ignoring another heated moment between them.

The doorbell rang and gave Cal an excuse

to leave the room before he took her comment seriously. The thought that Izzy wanted possession of any part of his body was arousing interest in certain areas that wasn't in keeping with their platonic agreement. 'I'll get it. It's probably the grocery shopping.'

With them both working and needing double the amount of food, they'd done their shopping online and left the front gates open for the home delivery to arrive. Izzy required proper nutritious meals and his recent casual approach to cooking ready meals and a microwave was no longer going to cut it.

The buzzer went again before he made it down the stairs.

'I'm coming,' he yelled to the dark figure outlined in the frosted glass who was clearly impatient to get to the next delivery.

As he unlocked the door to the outside world again, the person waiting for him made him want to slam the door shut and lock himself away with Izzy again.

'Hi, Cal.' That was it. With just two words Janet was back in his world, blowing it completely apart.

'Aren't you going to ask me in?' Her audacity in thinking she could smile at him as though she hadn't ripped his heart out of his chest and stomped on it rendered him speechless.

Apparently, that was invitation enough for her to push past him. Easily done with the considerable weight she was now wielding with her heavily pregnant belly. She'd be due any day now, but the thought no longer brought the same sadness it once had.

'I hope they brought those cheesy cracker things I wanted. I have a hankering for something savoury and salty.' Naturally this was the moment Izzy's pregnancy cravings kicked in and sent her foraging for goodies. She stopped dead at the bottom of the stairs and came face to face with Janet. 'What do you want?'

There was no question that his ex was only here because she wanted something from him. Under the circumstances he didn't think he should be expected to waste time on pleasantries and small talk. He had nothing to say to her.

Janet looked Izzy up and down with the same undisguised contempt she'd always done. Only now Cal could see it for what it was—jealousy. He'd loved Janet body and soul but after how she'd treated him his eyes were open to the ugliness she wore on the inside. Izzy was honest, and kind, and all those things Janet wasn't.

'I've come for the rest of my things.' She made her way past Izzy as though she was perfectly entitled to roam where she pleased.

Cal took off after her, a frown burrowing into his brow as he envisaged her rifling through Izzy's belongings and upsetting her. 'I'm pretty sure you took everything.'

It had made quite an impact to come home from work to find empty closets and drawers and spaces where some of their joint possessions had once resided. He'd been one step away from calling the police to report a burglary when he'd found her note. The one ending their relationship and destroying the dream of having a family together.

'I want the baby's things,' she insisted, and walked on into the nursery.

'You're kidding.' Did she really not think how much this would hurt him by taking away that last connection, or did she simply not care? Given her past behaviour, Cal presumed it to be the latter.

The pressure of Izzy's hand at his lower

back reminded him that someone did understand the significance of this to him and cared about it. Now he just wanted Janet to take any reminder of her out of his life for good.

'There's no point in wasting all this. It's not as though you're going to need it.' She went around the room, helping herself to the toys and bits and pieces dotted around the room and tossing them into the crib.

He was close to correcting her and informing her he did have a use for it, but he glanced at Izzy, who looked as horrified as he was, and she shook her head, making it known she didn't want a protest. Though Janet didn't deserve to walk away victorious, it was clear Izzy wanted Janet out at whatever price it took, instead of prolonging his agony.

The unwanted surprise appearance did prove one thing to Cal. He didn't, couldn't love her any more and he hoped that once she'd taken every last trace of their relationship away he'd forget all about her.

'Is Darren keeping a tight hold of the purse-strings? I don't blame him.' Cal had never denied Janet anything so perhaps she was missing being that pampered princess who'd once resided here. The thought of a possible rift didn't bring him any pleasure when their relationship had come at the price of his. Although he wasn't beyond making a dig.

'No,' she snapped, much too defensively for Cal to believe her. 'These were bought for the baby so I'm taking them for the baby.'

'Chosen by me and paid for by me.' More fool him for doing it and ending up here fighting over ownership of furniture for a baby that wasn't his.

'So you don't want him to have anything?' Janet cradled her bump and played a lament on his heartstrings. She was having a boy, a child he'd once seen himself playing football with and spending that father/son bonding time together as he'd done with his dad. He'd wanted that baby to have everything but that was when Cal had believed he'd be the one to see him make use of it all.

'I didn't say that, Janet.' If she was here for an argument he wasn't going to give her one because he no longer had the passion to fight. Not with her, anyway.

'In that case, you can start dismantling

everything and take it down to the car. *She can help you.*' Janet's inclusion of Izzy in her demands was where Cal drew the line.

'No, she won't. Where's Darren? He can help with the heavy lifting.' It said a lot about the man that he'd let Janet come in here alone. Darren was a coward, along with the other names Cal had assigned to him over the months for not stepping up for the woman he'd got pregnant and allowed to carry on a relationship with someone else.

'He's waiting in the van. He didn't want a scene.'

'If he wants the furniture he can get his backside in here and help. I'm not doing it on my own and Izzy's not either.' He was already on his knees, unscrewing the sides of the cot for easier removal. The purchases he'd made when he'd been so excited for the future now held nothing but resentment for him. He was only sorry he'd promised it to Izzy and had to go back on his word.

Janet glared at Izzy, who was hovering in the doorway, then at the new pots of paint and finally at Cal's bottom where Izzy had left her mark.

'Oh. My. Goodness. You two are moving

in together?' She laughed as she finally took in the scene.

'We are but it's not what you think.' Their set-up was none of Janet's business.

'That's priceless, making out as though I'm the bad person here when you two were carrying on behind my back the whole time. I knew there was something going on between you. Perhaps that's why I was driven to Darren.'

There was no way he was going to let her play the injured party and deflect the responsibility of her actions onto him and Izzy when they'd done nothing wrong.

'In case you've forgotten, you're the guilty one here. The decision to cheat on me and lie about the baby was entirely down to you. Now, I suggest that, to avoid any more unpleasantness, you go and wait in the van and send Darren in to collect whatever you believe you're still entitled to. After that I don't want to see or hear from either of you ever again.' He was trying to hold the emotion back and as a result he sounded menacingly in control. It was deceptive but hopefully effective because he didn't want to subject Izzy to any more of this toxicity.

Once Janet was gone they could start with a clean slate in whatever capacity she'd allow him to participate in her life. It had to be an improvement on being the sap Janet had taken him for when they were starting from a place of honesty.

This was the first time he'd had a chance to vent about what Janet had done to him and she simply puffed herself up with indignation and stomped away rather than admit to being in the wrong.

Cal set to work dismantling what was left of the nursery, so Darren could take it away without further discussion. There was nothing left to say except to apologise to Izzy for dragging her into this whole nightmare with him. His desire for a family had brought him nothing but trouble.

Izzy managed to hold her tongue until the furniture and unwanted guests had left the premises. She'd never been the woman's greatest fan but the nerve of Janet to come here and lay claim to everything ranked her the lowest of the low.

'I'm so sorry, Cal. That was just...' Heartless. Cruel. Cold. All of the above '...unbelievable.' It was heart-wrenching to see him slumped against the half-painted wall, sitting on the floor of the empty nursery. Janet's actions and manner tonight gave her some insight into how she'd treated him at the end of their relationship and it wasn't a pretty picture.

There was no justification for treating someone like Cal, who was kindness personified, in that manner. There wasn't a flicker of doubt in Izzy's mind that as a fiancé he'd been anything other than as loving and supportive as he was as a friend.

'You shouldn't have had to witness that, Iz.' He hung his head, clearly embarrassed at how things had panned out in front of her, but she was more concerned about how tonight's events had affected him.

'No, Janet should never have waltzed in here the way she did. I can't believe she had the audacity to turn up with Darren and take what didn't belong to her.' It was rubbing salt into the deep wound she'd inflicted, as though she never wanted it to heal.

Cal picked up a soft, cuddly sheep that had been left behind. 'It does look as though I've been burgled. At least she left Lamby behind. I've had him since I was a kid.'

He gave a sad smile that demanded she immediately hug him, but he couldn't manage to hug her back.

'I think he's had a lucky escape if you ask me. Who wants to live with a horror like that? Lamby will be much happier here with us. White furniture's too impractical anyway. Give it a week or two and everything she took will be permanently stained with puke and poo. She'll regret it someday.'

Nothing she could say would ever ease his pain, but she was here if he need her to jolly him along or keep him busy if he started to dwell on things again. It would've been so much worse if he'd have been left here in this shell of a nursery alone.

'I hope you're right.' Even so close she could sense him withdrawing from her when they needed one another more than ever.

'Next time we have a day off we could go shopping. I'm past the danger stage, touch wood, and I'd like to get organised. I'd appreciate your help in pointing me in the right direction to get what we need.' It was her attempt at including him more in this pregnancy, to give him something to look forward to, but she was taking a chance her good intentions might upset him further. The last thing she wanted to do was drag him around baby shops if it was all still too raw for him.

'I do happen to know of all the best recommendations when it comes to safety and quality.'

'I don't doubt it,' she said with a small laugh. He was so meticulous and thorough in everything he did. Assessing every possible risk was part of his job.

'She dumped me with a note taped to the fridge, you know. All those years living together, making plans for the future, and I wasn't worthy of a proper conversation. No apology, no explanation. "I'm leaving you for Darren. The baby's not yours, it's his." I mean, what could I have possibly done to deserve that? I spent weeks, months racking my brain, trying to figure out what I'd done wrong. Did I neglect her, had I become too clingy? Was I too boring or working too much? I'm still none the wiser after tonight.' His eyes were glistening with unshed tears Izzy wished she could wipe away.

'If anything good can come out of this it's that you can see this is none of your fault. Janet wouldn't have hesitated in casting up your faults if she could've blamed you for her behaviour. She has no excuse. The cheating, the lies, using the baby to get what she wanted—it's all on her. You were unlucky to have ever met her.' From now on they should concentrate on the future, instead of looking back.

'It still happened and it's not something I can easily forgive or forget.'

It was so uncharacteristic of Cal to be so despondent, but she knew from experience you had to hit rock bottom before you could claw your way back up again. Surveying the abandoned nursery, surely, he'd found his.

'No one would expect you to but please don't let her continue to ruin your life. Think of this as a new start. Now you're completely free from Janet and everything associated with her. I appreciate you, even if she doesn't.' From tomorrow Izzy was going to do everything in her power to help him move on with her.

CHAPTER SIX

'CAL, WE HAVE enough stuff to open our own shop.' Izzy glanced around the newly refurbished nursery, imagining their two little ones here.

They'd left it a couple of days after Janet's surprise visit before venturing out to replace the items she'd purloined. Even then Izzy had waited until Cal brought up the subject, instead of pushing him into a situation that might have made him uncomfortable. He'd been her personal shopper, pointing out the best products to suit her requirements, and she'd chosen the colours and theme for the room.

Unsurprisingly, Cal had insisted on paying for everything, though she'd sworn to pay him back somehow. Retail therapy had helped him cast off the shadow that had fallen over him after a certain someone had briefly come back into his life.

It was important for her to include him in these decisions for the babies so he'd stop hovering on the periphery of this pregnancy and become more involved. He was good at the practical aspects, such as the redecorating, but he'd yet to express his feelings about the situation. He was bound to have doubts and fears for their future just as she had, and it wasn't going to do any good keeping them bottled up. She didn't want to find out there were problems too late, the way she had with Gerry. That had been devastating enough but now there were children to think about too.

It wasn't going to serve anyone well if Cal maintained that emotional detachment when the babies were born. Especially when Izzy knew how much love he had to give. She only had a few months to convince him she wasn't Janet and it was safe for him to open his heart again.

'We'll have to get used to it. Twins are going to come with a lot of baggage and mess.' His immaculate home was going to be disrupted by two demanding, messy little beings. She didn't want it to come as a shock after he'd spent every spare minute putting the furniture together to complete this show-room nursery of her dreams.

They'd gone for an underwater theme, the room now festooned with cartoon sea crea-tures featuring on matching mobiles above the cribs and on the bedding. It was the kind of lovingly put-together room she wished she'd had as a child, instead of the generic spare bedrooms she'd always been desig-nated. When the children were old enough to choose their own décor, she'd make sure their rooms were tailor-made to suit their in-dividual interests and personalities so they never felt like interlopers, the way she had. Their home had to be somewhere they felt safe, wanted and surrounded by people who loved them.

'You know we're going to take over this house?' She eyed the boxes containing the highchairs and baby-walkers they wouldn't use for a while but which were already tak-ing up space.

'Trust me, I know exactly what chaos I've invited into my home.' He didn't sound com-pletely thrilled at the prospect but the smirk ghosting on his lips suggested he'd accepted the consequences.

After Janet's stunt she wouldn't have blamed him for changing his mind about sharing his house with anyone again. In the same position she might've decided it preferable to live on her own instead of inviting another pregnant woman to stay. To Cal's credit, he hadn't waivered in his decision to have her move in. He was reliable in that way and it was part of the reason she'd made a big decision regarding the twins.

'Cal? I have something to ask you.'

'Ask away.' He'd finished installing a night light that played a lullaby and projected moving images of seahorses and jellyfish around the walls. Izzy thought she might start sleeping in here herself if he made it any more appealing.

'Feel free to say no…you're under no obligation…but I was wondering if you'd consider being my birthing partner?' From the second that blue line had appeared on the pregnancy test she'd been determined to do it all on her own because she hadn't seen any other option. These past weeks Cal had shown her he was there for her day or night.

Although she didn't want to rely on him too heavily, with the twins on the way it was clear there were going to be more appointments, more risks involved, and these were times when it would be good to have someone holding her hand. It was also her plan to have him there to bond immediately with the babies and fall in love with them the second he saw them.

'You mean, like, be there at the birth?' Cal stopped tinkering long enough to come towards her, making her stomach flip. She couldn't tell if it was her hormones reacting to having him close or the babies letting her know they approved of the idea.

'Yeah. I thought you might like to be there.' She didn't have a partner or family member invested in her pregnancy, and Cal was the only person who had a right to be present in the delivery room with her.

'If that's what you want.' There was no indication that was what *he* wanted, but she was working on eventually teasing that information out of him.

'Just so we're clear, that doesn't entitle you to boss me about.' This role didn't give him carte blanche to interfere, and she'd remain the independent woman she'd always been.

'Okay, no pregnancy boot camp. I promise not to attempt to take over in any way. Although I hope that doesn't mean we can't discuss things like your birth plan or what sort of pain relief you'd prefer. It's good to look at all available options and work out what's best for you.'

At least he was thinking ahead on her behalf and it gave her hope that he wasn't going to leave her in the lurch when she'd need him most. Even if it was only on a practical level so far.

'You can help me draw up a suitable list of names too. Although I am putting my foot down now and saying no to suggestions of Bill and Ben, Pinky and Perky or any other such monikers.'

'I'm guessing that rules out This One and That One, too,' he said with a grin, but she knew he'd take the job seriously.

If there was one thing Izzy could guarantee her babies it was that they'd have somewhere to call home, and Cal had played a huge part in making that happen. No matter how reluctantly.

* * *

Cal walked into the office as Izzy was rubbing her hand across her chest with that pained expression on her face again. He set a tall glass of milk and a packet of antacids on the table before her. 'For the heartburn.'

She'd been getting a lot of that recently and particularly at night if the sounds of her pacing her bedroom were anything to go by.

As a result, she was becoming tired and irritable but as she refused to take time for extra rest, all they could do was wait for the symptoms to gradually ease as the pregnancy progressed.

It was difficult trying to look out for her best interests and avoid becoming a nag. There was a fine line between offering advice and interfering, and he knew he was currently straddling it. Especially since she'd asked him to be more involved as her birthing partner. She would've known he'd take that privileged position seriously and it wasn't something she'd assign to him on a whim. He was surprised when it had taken her so long to share the news about the pregnancy with him.

Cal wasn't the sort of man, or doctor, who

thought pregnant women should necessarily be wrapped up in cotton wool but sometimes there was cause to be concerned. Multiple pregnancy carried a higher risk of complications anyway but as he spent the working day alongside Izzy he knew how hard she worked and the high-octane, high-stress-level environment she did it in.

'What would I do without you?' Izzy batted her eyelashes at him and accepted the prescribed treatment.

'I think you'd manage pretty well,' he muttered, refusing to get drawn back into that role of faithful servant he'd become during Janet's pregnancy. It had hurt that much more when it had all been taken away from him, knowing she'd been taking advantage of his devotion and making a fool out of him. He wasn't going to let that happen twice in his lifetime.

'It was a joke, Cal. We both know I could do this without you.' In case he'd doubted it, Izzy emphasised the fact he was dispensable and reinforced the notion that neither of them should get too comfortable about their situation.

'Have you spoken to Mac yet?' There was

no point in being bitter about things now, so he moved them on to more practical, less emotive matters.

She'd been taking her time informing their bosses about the pregnancy, probably because she was afraid they'd ground her pretty soon. Working as ground crew overseeing hospital transfers might not be the job she'd signed up for, but there were too many health and safety risks involved professionally and personally to keep it secret for much longer.

'Yes. He's leaving it down to me to make the decision regarding when to take my maternity leave. Very sneaky, I thought. That way I can't complain when I'm forced to bail out. I suppose it depends on how huge I end up too. If I'm incubating two baby elephants in here, my bulk could stop the helicopter from lifting off the ground at all.'

Mac had been smart to put the ball back in Izzy's court because she would never jeopardise the safety of her crew over her pride. At least it was out in the open now and, bless her, her 'normal' clothes already seemed to be a bit snug. Her pride or denial that she was putting on weight couldn't last for ever.

Eventually she'd have to cave in and buy some maternity wear for a little comfort. It was rare for a multiple pregnancy to go to full term so there was no predicting how this one would advance or what toll it would take on her. He did know he'd be relieved when she made the decision not to go up in the air any more, for her own good and his peace of mind.

'We've got a call.' Mac sounded the alarm for the rest of the crew to get moving, everyone pulling on their flight gear as they made their way to the waiting helicopter. Izzy had that familiar rush of adrenaline that came with every call, reminding her that she had an important part to play in every one of these life-or-death calls.

'Fifty-two-year-old woman thrown from her horse. May have sustained head and neck injuries.' Cal repeated the details of the patient requiring their assistance.

'We'll need to set down somewhere close to the site. There's an empty field next to the jumps there.' He gave instructions to the pilot over the headset for a suitable green space to land, clear of buildings, people and anything else that could impede their arrival.

Izzy was trying to focus on the ground rushing up to meet them, estimating how long it would take them to reach those in danger. However, the noise and vibration of the chopper as they raced to the scene was beginning to affect her. Before the pregnancy all the shaking and shouting that went on prior to landing had served to heighten the thrill of hitting the ground running.

Today, though, her body was responding altogether differently to the experience. Every shudder, every drop in altitude had her stomach lurching. She didn't know if it was a sudden and impractical bout of travel sickness or delayed morning sickness. One thing was sure, though, these babies seemed to be protesting about the current mode of transport. Unfortunate when it was also her place of work.

Izzy would never intentionally put any patient in jeopardy due to potential personal issues. She was hoping this was a one-off. If not, she was going to have to hang up her flight suit much earlier than she'd anticipated. She could hardly go running to someone's rescue if she was going to be violently ill every time she was on a call-out.

The wind generated by the chopper blades flattened the grass around them and Izzy and Cal jumped out. She let him run on ahead in the hope he wouldn't witness her vomit stop at the hedge and pulled the water bottle from the kit on her back to wash her mouth out. Except when she was ready to carry on he was glaring back at her. He didn't have to say anything for her to know he wasn't happy she was continuing to work as usual despite her discomfort. In other circumstances she might have accused him of pregnancy discrimination but given her current state she could see he had a point.

'What? Drinking a full glass of milk before getting shaken about was never a good idea.' She had an excuse this time but the next time he'd call her bluff. He could pull rank on her and play the doctor card to force her into co-operating. Anything more serious than some nausea and she'd put herself on bed rest. She was stubborn, but she was also a mum-to-be and she was learning what that entailed.

Cal opened his mouth to say something, probably to scold her, then took off again without saying a word towards the congregation in the adjacent field. It was almost worse having understanding colleagues trusting she knew her own body well enough to make the call when it came to cutting back on work, rather than have them making decisions on her behalf. Almost. Only because she'd have no right to rant and rave at anyone when the crew took off without her.

For now, she was making the most of still having the job she was trained to do, rushing towards someone relying on her and Cal to get them safely delivered to the nearest hospital.

He introduced himself to the gentleman kneeling on the ground next to the woman who'd apparently suffered the fall. 'Can you tell me what happened?'

Izzy knelt on the wet grass beside them and began to unpack the medical equipment they were liable to require.

'I found her like this. When she didn't come home for lunch I came to look for her.' It was clear the man was trying not to panic but he'd done the right thing by not moving her and phoning for help straight away.

'She hasn't gained consciousness since?' A sign that she could have suffered a head injury from the fall or that the horse might have kicked out at her.

'She's made the odd moaning sound, but she hasn't woken up.'

That was something at least. 'How long ago did you find her?'

'About fifteen, maybe twenty minutes ago.' The man was clinging to his wife's hand and Izzy prayed this had a happy ending. Since finding out she was going to have a family of her own she'd become much more sentimental concerning the partners and children involved on the cases. Now, with the love in her heart for the babies she was carrying and having Cal there for her, she better understood the impact of illness or injury on loved ones.

'What's her name?'

'Agnes.'

'Agnes, can you hear me?' Cal tried to garner a response as Izzy set about getting her ready to be moved.

There was a faint groan to reassure them that Agnes was clinging to consciousness.

'We think you've hit your head in a fall so it's very important you stay still until we get that neck stabilised. We're going to give you some pain relief then we'll put a brace around your neck to keep you immobile. You might be uncomfortable but the sooner we can get you stable here the quicker we can get you into the helicopter and on your way to the hospital. Okay?'

She gave another groan in response and though she tried to bat them away at times they managed to get the brace and backboard on her.

'We're going to take her to the local hospital if you want to meet us there. The trauma team already knows we're on our way.' Cal relayed their intentions to the husband.

It was at least forty minutes there by road, but they could do it in less than fifteen by air. Part of the reason they'd been dispatched for this call.

When Izzy got to her feet to transport the trolley over to the helicopter she stumbled, a tad unbalanced as the world around her began to spin. Thankfully she was holding

onto the side of the stretcher, which pre-
vented her from landing in a heap in the
middle of the field.

The dizzy spell passed as quickly as it had
begun but she could already feel Cal's eyes
burning a hole into her.

'I'm fine,' she mouthed as they rushed towards the chopper, but knew deep down this
was the beginning of the end for her out in
the field.

All systems were go as they hooked Agnes
up to the monitors on board and radioed in
their ETA.

'I've got this.' Cal nodded towards the
jump seat, indicating he wanted her to sit
this one out. There was nothing to be gained
from arguing and detracting his attention
from the patient when he was the medical
lead and had the final say here.

Although she would challenge him if she
categorically believed he was wrong, on this
occasion she had to concede to his authority.
She was no use to Cal or Agnes swaying on
her feet and ready to pass out at any second.

'There's a protein bar and a juice in my
bag. Take them.' Cal went back on his word
not to boss her around, but she needed it. She

might have been insisting she could carry on as normal, but some things had to change. Including skipping meals and risking her blood pressure dropping too low.

In the past all that had meant was having dinner later than usual. Now it could put their missions in jeopardy. They couldn't take the chance of her fainting in the middle of treating a patient or when they were in the air. From now on she was going to have to plan and prepare for all eventualities to prevent this from happening again. That was if she was ever allowed to fly again for the duration of the pregnancy when they'd have to log a record of this incident.

Regardless that she wasn't hungry or thirsty, she followed Cal's instruction so when they landed on the helipad on the hospital roof she was feeling more like herself.

'Okay, Agnes. That's us at the hospital now. The staff know we're coming so they'll be waiting for us to transfer you into their care.' It was Cal who talked her through the proceedings as she continued to drift in and out of consciousness in the hope some of the information would filter through and the change in surroundings wouldn't be too much of a shock.

Izzy took her place on the other side of the stretcher from Cal and they wheeled her out to the waiting trauma team. Cal reeled off Agnes's personal details and his observations and once they'd handed over responsibility, the air crew was able to breathe again.

Not that Cal would let her get away with having a wobble on his watch without an investigation. 'You're going home for a proper meal and complete bed rest.'

It wasn't the worst proposition she'd ever had, and it was one she'd welcome. There wasn't a choice anyway when she was living with him. He'd insist on cooking her a nutritious meal and probably escort her to her room to make sure she followed his advice this time.

'Yes, sir.' She clicked her heels together and saluted, the teasing an attempt to reassure him he could stop fretting.

It was unfortunate that the sharp, sudden movement tilted the world around her all over again. That slight spinning sensation she'd experienced earlier evolved into a vortex sucking the oxygen out of the atmosphere and drawing her into its core. She couldn't keep her focus on any one point, including Cal's concerned face.

He sounded so far away as he called out her name. Then she was drifting away, the darkness that was calling her home. She was falling, her body crumpling under her as she gave in to unconsciousness, but the last thing she remembered was Cal's arms around her and a feeling of weightlessness as she was carried off into the unknown.

CHAPTER SEVEN

'Izzy? Fizz?' Cal called out to her the second he saw her wobble. He'd known something was wrong and wished he'd asked the hospital staff to send transport for her too.

He could see the unfocused gaze and reached her a millisecond before she passed out. With a volley of expletives to alert the rest of the air crew, he caught her in his arms and rushed her off in the direction the hospital staff had gone.

Everything in his training told him it was probably wasn't anything more than a faint. Nothing unusual for a pregnant woman, especially one who hadn't been eating properly and was overdoing it. It didn't prevent him from reacting on an emotional level as he witnessed her collapse. All those irrational fears that he was going to lose another loved one came rushing to the surface, making him act as though her life depended on it.

Even pregnant with twins, she seemed so fragile in his arms, completely dependent on him to get her to safety. Whatever past hurt had been preventing him from bonding with these babies was immaterial compared to what he was feeling now, faced with the possibility of losing them for ever. He was their father after all and resisting that connection was pointless when nothing in the world could alter that fact. Worry was simply a part of fatherhood he'd never outrun, and when it could all be snatched away from him at any moment he didn't know why he was trying. He should be making the most of every second of it.

By the time he'd whisked Izzy down to the emergency department she was thankfully beginning to come around.

'Sasha, I need some help here.' He commandeered an empty cubicle and called over one of the nurses he recognised from their transfers.

With a gentle hand he manoeuvred Izzy's head to rest on the hospital bed, grateful he'd caught her before she'd hit the ground and perhaps given herself a concussion on top of everything else.

'What's happened to Iz?' One of the benefits of rushing emergencies through was that at least they were familiar faces around here. Although given the capacity in which Sasha knew them she'd be forgiven for thinking some catastrophe had befallen the helicopter.

'She fainted up on the roof while we were doing a handover. I should probably tell you she's pregnant with twins, in her second trimester.' Cal could see the surprise on the nurse's face but as she didn't push any further he refrained from sharing any more of Izzy's personal information. Although he imagined people were going to find out he was the father sooner or later.

'Did she hit her head at any point?'

'No.' He was confident about that at least, thanks to his quick reflexes and the close eye he'd been keeping on her.

'Izzy? Can you hear me? It's Sasha in Accident and Emergency. It would really help us if you could open your eyes, sweetie.' Whilst she tried to rouse Izzy, Cal scooted over to the sink to wet some paper towels.

'Cal? Where's Cal?'

He heard her confused mumble and hurried back to her bedside to place the cold compress on her forehead. 'I'm here, Fizz.'

She was trying to sit up, but he placed a hand on her chest and gently eased her back. 'You fainted. We need you to rest up for a while.'

If she wouldn't listen to him, perhaps the staff here could convince her.

'The babies?' Her first thoughts went to her bump, along with her hands.

Cal understood that sense of terror, that utter feeling of dread and powerlessness because that's exactly what had happened to him when he'd seen her drop like a stone. He might not be Izzy's romantic partner, but he was still entitled to worry about all of them. It was clear he was the only one they had in their lives to rely on and he didn't want to let any of them down.

'I'm sure they're fine. You haven't been out long, and I brought you straight here.' He squeezed her hand, although he knew it wouldn't do much to reassure her in the circumstances.

Her chin began to wobble, her throat bobbed up and down each time she swallowed, and Cal could see how much she was desperately trying to hold back tears. With a cough to clear his throat he looked to Sasha for help. 'We can get an ultrasound to check everything's okay with the babies, right? Just to put Izzy's mind at ease.'

Sasha smiled at him in that way that said she knew he needed the confirmation too. 'Of course. We're going to check your blood pressure and take some bloods first, Izzy, so we can see if there's anything that caused you to faint. Have you been thirstier or needing to urinate more than usual?'

'No. Why, do you think it could be gestational diabetes?' Izzy was one step ahead of the nurse because of the symptoms she was describing, but Cal was sure it was something much simpler. Her blood sugar level was probably too low, rather than the opposite.

'We're just being thorough in our investigations but if you haven't noticed any symptoms then it's not likely to be GD. We'll do all the tests anyway.'

'She hasn't been eating properly.' He was ready for Izzy to call him a snitch, but she was waiting for Sasha's opinion on continu-

f busied themselves around
g her settled for her upcom-
emained stubbornly in place.
one and she was successfully
the machines checking her
leaned in and whispered, 'I

u mean?'
he side of his nose. 'As long as
ght and promise not to get you
r fellow patients over-excited
l dispensation to stay outside

she should be magnanimous
he was fine here on her own.
vas relieved to have him with
ger.

winge of guilt every time Izzy
l's flight suit draped over the
air when she knew if it wasn't
e at home, relaxing after his

at I'd call *haute cuisine*,' she
they both finished the unap-
of hospital food they'd been

---

ing her casual attitude to mealtimes during pregnancy.

'The thing to remember, Izzy, is that during pregnancy you're sharing your blood supply with your baby, and in your case two babies. I would recommend carrying snacks with you. Going without food will affect you more now.'

'Thanks, Sasha. I guess I'm going to have to start listening to my body more,' Izzy said, looking a little more reassured that there was no reason this pregnancy shouldn't go full term without any further complications. She probably just needed some rest and TLC, which Cal was always offering to help her with.

He knew their relationship had gone far beyond friendship, despite his intention not to get too close, but he was afraid to acknowledge it. There was so much on the line he couldn't risk what they already had together. The best he could probably hope for was that she'd continue to let him play a part in her life.

The whole event had given Izzy quite a fright. If it was a sign she should take things easier she was going to make sure she took heed of it rather than go through this again. Thank goodness she'd been given another peek at her little jellybeans to make sure they hadn't suffered during her dizzy spell. She supposed it was too much to ask if they could install one of those machines at home, so she could obsessively check on them for the next few months.

'We're going to move you onto the ward for the night, Izzy. The blood tests have shown signs of anaemia so we're going to have to get you started on some iron supplements, and your blood pressure's quite low too. I suspect that's what caused the fainting today and I'd like to keep you in overnight so we can keep an eye on that.' The doctor hadn't given her any chance to disagree and though she understood the precautions she simply wanted to go home.

'Can't you wheel me out the back door and take me home with you?' she suggested to Cal as he followed her to the ward, holding her hand as the porter manoeuvred her around corridor corner.

He was pale, she'd put him through a lot today. She was sure it had been no mean feat, car[...] the roof, [...] side sinc[...] in this o[...] the whole [...] though he [...] as worrie[...] and she c[...]

'Believe [...] they're be[...] So far, he [...] would be [...] ture, but s[...] he might i[...] care at hom[...] going to ha[...] thought of [...] warmth and [...] house. Thei[...]

'You shou[...] have someth[...] ting sick on [...] him to go. E[...] patients and [...] treating, shri[...] ing up those [...] did go and le[...]

As the sta[...] her bed, getti[...] ing stay, Cal [...] Once they'd [...] hooked up t[...] progress, Ca[...] have contact[...]

'What do [...] He tapped [...] I keep out of [...] or any of yo[...] I've got spec[...] visiting hou[...]

Izzy knev[...] and tell him [...] In truth, she [...] her a little l[...]

There was [...] glanced at [...] back of his [...] for her he'[...] shift.

'It's not [...] apologised [...] petising p[...]

served. It made her appreciate Cal's efforts in the kitchen every night even more.

'I'm just thankful she took pity on me and donated the unwanted meal to a good home.' He certainly hadn't turned his nose up at the free dinner offered to him from the trolley after being rejected by a more discerning diner. Izzy thought it was indicative of how ravenous he was when she'd had to force down every mouthful. Then again, she was too stressed and anxious about the babies to have any sort of appetite.

Despite the reassurances and precautions, there was still a long way to go and plenty of time for other, more serious complications to occur.

'Hey, don't you go getting all maudlin on me.' Cal set his empty plate beside hers on the table across her bed.

'Sorry, I'm not much company for you.'

'Would you prefer it if I left you alone?' The determined set of his jaw told her he seriously believed she might be better on her own than have him with her.

'No,' she said, much too quickly, and grabbed his hand. All that would do was make her even more miserable and give her more time to dwell on all the negatives of the situation when he was the only one who could give her a much-needed boost.

'Good. Otherwise there'd be no one here to make sure you eat up all of your fruit salad.' He lifted the dish of chopped fruit and pulled his chair closer to the bed. 'Now, are you going to open up or do I have to make aeroplane noises?'

When he began moving the spoon towards her mouth she complied by eating it, touched that he cared so much about her. She couldn't remember anyone nursing her when she was ill.

In the shared foster homes, the parents had been afraid of any viruses spreading to the rest of the children and at the first sign of sickness she'd been quarantined in her room. She'd thought all those images she'd seen in TV shows of worried parents mopping the brows of fevered offspring were pure fiction. Until Cal had refused to leave her bedside and she understood what she'd been missing. To have someone who cared about her well-being more than their own was alien to her but something she could easily become accustomed to.

'Do I get a prize if I finish it all?' she asked before accepting the last morsel. In normal circumstances she might have been liable to throw the food at someone trying to feed her like a baby, but Cal wasn't trying to patronise her, he was trying to lift her spirits and make sure she got some sustenance. Okay, she was enjoying the attention too.

'Why, is there something I can tempt you with?' He waggled his eyebrows suggestively at her and made her laugh. It was good to have someone around who was so good at distracting her when she needed it and, boy, was he a distraction. There had been a few moments between them when she'd been convinced they were going to give in to temptation again. She'd ached for it, but Cal was always the one to pull back from the brink. It had been on her say so, of course, one of the conditions of her moving in, but it seemed she was powerless against her own hormones.

'I want you in my bed,' she said, enjoying the shock on his face as she leaned forward and helped herself to the last spoonful of fruit.

Izzy patted the space next to her on the bed.

'The staff have been very accommodating, but I think that might be pushing things too far,' he said with a cheeky glint in his eye.

'I won't tell if you don't.'

After years of knowing and teasing each other it suddenly felt more real. As though the flirting was going to lead somewhere. It was probably because they were both exhausted mentally and physically that they were letting this spark between them flare into life again. Beyond the comfort and support Cal represented, that attraction also lingered, on her part at least, but she knew nothing could come of it.

She was sure this fancy would pass once the babies were safely here and she didn't feel so vulnerable. More than likely she was confusing his kindness for something that wasn't there but had been lacking her entire life. Love.

Cal didn't wait for a second invitation, only pausing to kick off his shoes. The instant he climbed onto the bed beside her and put his arm around her she snuggled into his chest with a sigh.

Perhaps it was because she was feeling vulnerable, or that they'd become so close lately, but Izzy felt compelled to share how important it was to have him there for her.

'You know, I usually can't bear anyone near me when I'm sick. I'm not used to it.'

'Not even Gerry?' It was probably difficult for Cal to understand when he'd been so considerate. Plus, it was his job, his duty of care to look after the sick and infirm.

Gerry wasn't a subject she liked to discuss with Cal for obvious reasons.

'He was on the road a lot and I think it was better for us both that he wasn't around if I was ill.' She gave a little laugh because she could see now how unreasonable she'd been at times. It was fine for her to lecture others on self-care when they weren't well, but she had no time for lying around feeling sorry for herself. She wouldn't have thanked Gerry for pandering to her either, thinking he'd have an ulterior motive for keeping on her good side. That was on top of her already ingrained need to contain the possible spread of infection.

Now Cal had shown her the sort of nurturing she'd been missing out on since the day she'd been born, and she swore her own children would know what it was to be loved and cherished every day of their lives.

'That's one of the many things I miss about not having my mum around.' Cal was absent-mindedly stroking her hair and Izzy closed her eyes, gave herself over to his tender touch.

'If I was sick she'd give up her whole day, no matter what she'd been doing beforehand, to spend it looking after me. She made the best chicken soup and brought it to me in bed. Nothing was too much trouble and she'd spend hours reading to me or playing board games with me. Even when I left home she'd rush over a pot of soup at the first sign of a sniffle. I guess you could say I was spoiled.' He gave a self-deprecating laugh but the picture he painted was more about a very special mother and son bond than an over-indulged brat.

'More loved, I'd say. Your mum sounds as though she was a lovely person.' It was easy to understand where he got his loving nature from and Izzy wasn't jealous of his idyllic-sounding upbringing.

'She was, as was Dad. Nothing was ever the same after they died. There was no one there to keep the rest of us together and it felt as though I'd lost the rest of my family along with them. My sisters moved away with their husbands and children and suddenly I was no longer a son, a brother or an uncle. I lost my sense of identity along with them. When Janet told me she was pregnant I had a role again. I was going to be a husband and father, that's why the loss was so great when she left. I lost myself along with her and the baby and it took me a long time to rediscover my identity as just Cal. I think that's why I'm finding it difficult relating to the role of being a father again. I don't want it to completely define who I am.'

The sadness in his voice made Izzy reach out and wrap her arms around his waist. It was clear he was afraid of committing again in case she took it all away from him again, the way Janet had.

'I know the Cal you were before all this happened and I promise I won't let you get cast adrift in all the excitement. I want you very much to be a part of everything.'

He gave a brief nod before changing the subject. 'What about you? You don't say much about your foster parents except that they live some distance away.'

'I've never been able to think of them as Mum and Dad, although they were the last couple to assume the roles. I never knew my birth parents and I was passed around a series of foster homes until I was old enough to go it alone. Some of the foster parents genuinely wanted to help kids in the system, others you could tell were only in it for the money, and more than a few simply weren't equipped to deal with those of us who had serious issues about our start in life. I know I acted up, pushing the boundaries to test how willing they were to keep me, and as a result I never stayed in one place too long. Theory proved.

'Meeting Helen changed things for me. She lived next door and became a real friend, the first I'd ever had. I was welcomed into her home as part of the family and I probably spent more time there, eating their food and talking over my problems with her, than in any one of my foster homes. I think that's why having my own family is so important to me. I want my children to have that love and stability I'd never had. While I'm grateful to those people who did take me in, I was never treated as a *proper* daughter. There was no real affection there and I knew it when I saw how Helen's parents interacted with her. I didn't have anyone who cared when I was sick, and I'm not used to having it now. I guess that's why I get cranky around people when I'm ill.'

'My poor Izzy. Yet you're willing to put up with me. I'm honoured.' He dropped a kiss on her head and Izzy wanted to remain cocooned here in this cubicle with him for ever.

'You're different. I'm—' She stopped herself just in time before the words *I'm in love with you* caught them both by surprise. 'I'm used to you.' She managed to cover her back before she spoiled the moment by saying something daft enough to lose him, her home and her future when he'd admitted he didn't feel the same way.

'That's good to know.' He chuckled, the vibration of his chest beneath her cheek having the opposite effect on her from the judder of the helicopter. Instead of upsetting her stomach, it was comforting.

They settled into an easy silence but that thinking time soon led her into more anxiety.

'Cal? I'm scared.' She shared her fears, watching for reassurance even when she knew he'd never abandon her or lie to her the way everyone else in her life had done. He'd shown her that today and every day since he'd found out about the babies, when most would have run from the responsibility.

He leaned down until they were nose to nose and she could see the sincerity in his eyes. 'I will never let anything happen to you. You mean too much to me.'

She was tired of fighting this thing between them. When he was looking at her with such adoration and longing she no longer knew why she was resisting the inevitable. Especially when she knew how good it felt to give in to those impulses.

She closed her eyes and tilted her chin up, inviting him to make that final decision and seal their fate. Only a second later she felt that soft pressure of his lips on hers bringing her whole body back to life. For once she was being true to herself and to her feelings and could only pray Cal was doing the same.

There was the worry he was only kissing her to comfort her but as he tangled his hand in her hair and strengthened that physical connection between them she knew better than to doubt his intentions. He'd opened up to her emotionally about his childhood and his fears and he wouldn't have done that unless he was thinking seriously about their future. Cal wanted her. All of her.

Izzy freed her mind from everything except how good it felt to be touching him again. Everything she wanted was there in his kiss—comfort, security, but most of all the intense passion she'd convinced herself had only existed in that one night. How wrong she'd been when he was pulling her close to his body, telling her how much he wanted her without saying a word. His lips captured hers again and again, his tongue teased hers until she thought she'd expire if he didn't give her more.

It also sent her heart monitor into overdrive, so he knew exactly what effect he was having on her. She felt his smile against her lips before he pulled away from her again.

'I should probably go before the nurses throw me out.' His voice was thick with desire as he shifted his weight on the mattress, but Izzy wasn't ready for him to leave apparently any more than he was.

'Can't you stay a little bit longer?' It was unlike her to be needy, but she was done with being alone when she could be in Cal's arms.

'You need your sleep. I'm keeping you awake.'

'In the best possible way. There's plenty of room for two.' She tried to convince him, though it was doubtful whether either of them would have a comfortable night with four of them essentially packed into one single bed.

'Nice try.' He sat up and arranged the pillows for her to lie down.

'I'll stay here until you fall asleep,' he whispered into her ear, spooning against her with his arm draped so casually across her waist one might've believed this was a nightly occurrence. It was a pleasant thought, even though she wanted more.

Izzy closed her eyes, a smile on her lips as exhaustion claimed her. She hadn't realised how much she needed or wanted Cal in her life until she couldn't imagine one without him in it.

CHAPTER EIGHT

CAL HAD BEEN like a kid on Christmas Eve, unable to settle, waiting for the call to go and pick Izzy up from the hospital. He'd ignored the cramp in his limbs, which had set in as he'd been lying on that hospital bed with her because he hadn't wanted to swap it for the luxury of his spacious king-size bed.

Home offered him peace, space and comfort in comparison but without Izzy it was hard to find any of that. He'd have happily slept all night with her pressed against his chest, dead arm and all, just to be close to her a while longer. That's when he knew he was in way over his head.

This was supposed to have been a gesture that he was committed to raising the babies with Izzy. Moving in together was never meant to have been more than a favour.

He'd certainly never intended to get as close to Izzy as he'd apparently become. It left him open to the same kind of emotional hurt he'd been through once too often. With her determination to include him every step of the way through this pregnancy she'd broken through those defences he'd imagined would keep his heart protected. When he thought losing her or the babies was a possibility he knew he'd become completely attached to the idea of their little family.

Yesterday had been stressful for them both but it must have taken a particular toll on Izzy for her to let him so close and to want him to stay. She'd always been a firecracker and independent to the point of being obstreperous, so it was an indication of just how much turmoil she'd been in for her to let him hold her.

Then there was the kiss. He'd been so overcome with compassion for her situation, gratitude for having her in his life and, well, love, there was nothing he could've done to prevent it from happening. When Izzy had kissed him back his whole body had sung out with sheer happiness that she'd wanted him too. It was only the rise in her blood pressure that had reminded him she was vulnerable, and he hadn't wanted to take advantage of that when he was the only person she had in her life. It would confuse her at a time when her whole world was in chaos and what she needed from him more was a sense of security and stability. Something she'd apparently been missing out on for some time.

She didn't have friends or family around and it was natural she should reach out for the nearest available substitute. He'd do well to remember that's all he was in the picture.

'Would you like me to hunt down a wheelchair to get you to the car?' Cal waited patiently as Izzy packed her newly prescribed medication and toiletries into the bag he'd brought for her.

She gave him a sidelong look. 'Would you like me to get a wheelchair to take *you* to the car?'

'Okay, okay. I was only trying to save you a walk.' He held his hands up in surrender. Secretly, he was pleased she was back to her fighting best. For him it was a better sign she was on the mend than her improved blood pressure and blood test results. Even if he'd miss his temporary position as chief hand-holder.

'I've been cooped up in bed too long. I need the exercise and some fresh air. Not to mention something to eat that doesn't resemble baby food. Can we stop somewhere on the way home?' She whispered the request, presumably to prevent offending anyone from hospital catering if they overheard.

'I can do better than that. I've stocked up on fresh fruit and vegetables and I'm going to cook you a veritable welcome-home feast. Anything your heart desires.' Cal bowed and grabbed her luggage before she insisted on carrying it herself.

From now on, he intended to provide her with wholesome, nutritious meals to ensure she wouldn't be lacking in any more essential vitamins or minerals. Avoiding any further upsetting overnight hospital stays.

'For now, I'd be happy if you took me home and put the kettle on.' Izzy softened a little towards him, slipping her arm through his and leaning against him for the duration of the short walk to the car.

'I think I can manage that.' He had worried that her defences had reassembled during the time since she'd last seen him and that she might have regretted their cosy bed-time cuddle session. On his return home, Cal's bed had suddenly seemed so vast and empty compared to that hospital trolley. Even more so than after Janet had left him. It was only with some considerable thought, com-paring that one spooning session with Izzy against years of sharing a bed with Janet, he realised proximity to someone didn't ac-tually constitute the nature of a close rela-tionship.

They'd gone through the motions together as a couple, but they'd never had that bond he had with Izzy. Which was probably why Janet had never approved of their friendship.

Yesterday, experiencing that pain and worry together and finally expressing some of the emotions they'd tried to keep locked down, had finally cemented their bond. Their only worry now should be making sure these babies were safely delivered into the world.

He unlocked the car, which he'd parked as close to the entrance as he dared, risking a fine to save Izzy an uphill walk to the car park. Instead of climbing into the passenger seat, as he'd expected, Izzy suddenly turned around and said, 'Thank you for everything, Calum,' and kissed him full on the lips.

He drove on autopilot, in a loved-up haze, back to the home they shared. The only place he knew both of them wanted to be, where they could close the door and re-create that cocoon. Where all they needed was each other.

Izzy had spent the rest of the week under house arrest as per Cal's orders. She knew it wasn't a control issue, she'd worked alongside Cal long enough to know he wasn't the kind of guy who needed to exert his authority every second of the day. However, he was compassionate and well mannered. Not usually qualities a woman would find irritating unless she was used to being fiercely independent.

She was going stir crazy forced to stay in one place for so long, not permitted to lift a finger to do anything. It was alien to her, being so cosseted that she didn't know how to deal with it. So she'd gone back to being her bolshie self, giving Cal a hard time and accusing him of suffocating her because deep down she was afraid of jumping his bones for paying her a bit of attention.

Not that he'd have let her expend that sort of energy, even if he had reciprocated these new feelings she'd been harbouring towards him. She'd thought that night in the hospital and that wonderful sensation of falling asleep in his arms had been the start of something more between them. Except he'd turned into her carer since then with no inclination towards anything other than nursing her.

He hadn't reacted to the kiss she'd given him when they'd left the hospital and so she'd consigned it to the list of bad decisions she'd made regarding suitable men. She'd taken his kindness and understanding and tried to sabotage the relationship they did have by taking it somewhere he might not have wanted it to go. What else could Cal have done when she'd made him get into her bed and poured her heart except to make her feel better? She'd provided the awkward element by attempting to extend that moment beyond the hospital walls.

Unfortunately, this imposed relaxation was having the opposite effect it was supposed to have on her. Instead of keeping her calm and chilled out, it was giving her too much time to obsess about everything that had happened recently or could happen in the near future.

She'd tried everything to distract her thoughts from Cal and what he was doing without her at work. Including watching so much trashy daytime television she wanted to scratch her eyes out. Taking up knitting hadn't helped either. There were so many holes in the simple squares she'd attempted to piece into a blanket it looked more like crochet.

Izzy lit on him the second she heard the key in the lock, desperate for some human company instead of the virtual kind. 'You should have texted to let me know you were on your way home. I could have had dinner in the oven for you.'

She felt like a nineteen-fifties housewife, waiting barefoot and pregnant for the centre of her universe to come home from work and give her life some meaning. She really needed to get back to work and do something useful. Never in a million years could she have pictured herself in the role of the happy housewife because she'd never imagined it existed. Although she'd go mad if she spent every day tied to the kitchen sink with no outside interests, she had to admit there was a certain appeal in sharing dinner and chores with a man who would happily put her on a pedestal.

'I wouldn't expect you to do that. You're supposed to be taking it easy.' Cal hung up his jacket and rolled up his shirtsleeves, preparing to go into the kitchen and start making dinner. He was one in a million and easy to take advantage of if you were an unscrupulous user like his ex. On the other hand, this total pampering deal made her feel uncomfortable because she didn't know what to do with herself.

'Cal, I've been taking it so easy I'm practically comatose. I'm fine. The midwife confirmed that at my last appointment. My blood pressure is where it should be, as are my iron levels. Besides, you've cooked and labelled enough food to see out the entire pregnancy. All I'd have to do is microwave it.' Given his history it was no wonder he was used to doing his Florence Nightingale bit, but he couldn't carry on in this vein or she'd burst a blood vessel from pent-up frustration.

'You say that as though it's a bad thing.'

'It's not that I don't appreciate all your effort to take care of me, Cal. I'm simply not used to it. You know I'm not the type to sit on my backside and let everyone run around after me, no matter what the circumstances. I'm going back to work on Monday and before you say anything I'll make sure it's as ground crew only.' Then she wouldn't get in anyone's way and could still remain part of the team. She wasn't asking his permission, but she did respect him enough to inform him of her decision.

He nodded. 'It's one hundred per cent your choice, Iz. All I wanted to do was fulfil my promise to take care of you and the babies.'

'I know.' And she loved him for it. If only his actions were based on more than a misplaced sense of duty.

'Look, why don't we go out for a meal?'

Izzy was tempted to ask if he meant as a date, but it was more likely to be a compromise, so she had to dampen down her initial excitement that they were making progress on their personal relationship.

'It would be nice to leave these four walls and pay a visit into civilisation.' Izzy also realised it would be the first time they'd gone out to a restaurant as anything other than work colleagues. She couldn't help but hope for the day when they did it as a couple, or even a family.

'It's a date, then. Give me ten minutes to shower and change and we'll hit the town.' Cal bounded up the stairs to freshen up, while Izzy did her best to get her fluttering pulse back under control.

'I get the impression our waiter thinks we're having some sort of clandestine affair,' Izzy whispered across the secluded, candlelit table, which had obviously been set to create a romantic scene.

Cal grinned at her, clearly amused by being ushered towards the dark corner with her, away from businessmen and noisy young families.

'Then maybe we should give him something to talk about.' He took her hand and lifted it to his mouth, brushing his lips across her fingers and making shivers dance their way across her skin. Her brain might have decided one or two kisses were probably best forgotten, but her body was keen to remind her of the intensity of sensations his touch alone could cause.

Whilst she tried to get her thoughts and rogue body parts under control, she noticed he'd gone quiet too. It really was time they were honest about what was happening between them on an emotional level.

'Cal, I think it's us who have something to talk about.'

For once he didn't pull away from her when they were veering towards the important issues affecting their relationship and held her hand fast in his.

'I know. We've kind of let things run away from us.' He was smiling, so it seemed he didn't totally regret those flashes of passion which kept flaring up between them.

'I just want to know where I stand. Where we stand, Cal.' She was putting everything they did have on the line by asking for that clarification, but they couldn't go on pretending they were able to suppress those urges for ever. The next time they gave in to them she knew she wouldn't be able to go back to being just friends. Not now love had become part of the equation for her.

It had come slowly, creeping in along with the friendship and passion they'd cultivated over time, but as she'd learned, ignoring her feelings didn't make them go away. If anything, it simply left them to spin out of control and with time running out before the babies came along, it was more important than ever to get some clarity on their relationship. She wanted to put down roots for her family but only if there was a strong, stable foundation available for them.

Of course, their waiter arrived back with their meals at the most inconvenient time, forcing them to break apart and lose that physical connection.

'Thanks.' Cal smiled politely at their server while Izzy did her best to hold her tongue until he left.

'I mean, we're going to be a family, whether you like it or not.' Weeks of pussyfooting around him in case she frightened him off by making him face the truth finally caught up with her and she ignored her delicious plate of Cajun chicken pasta to confront this head on.

Cal hung his head and sighed. 'I'll be the first to admit I haven't been the most excited father-to-be, but after Janet I'm a bit more cautious about the idea of family.'

'No kidding.' Izzy speared a piece of pasta and cursed that woman for making their lives more complicated than they needed to be. If it hadn't been for her cruel treatment of such a wonderful man, she and Cal might have settled down together by now and be looking forward to the birth of their children. Not fearing the event would trigger more betrayal or heartbreak.

They both ate in silence, but Izzy couldn't enjoy her dinner when it was overpowered by the taste of bitterness in her mouth.

Eventually Cal broke first, giving her some insight to the workings of his troubled mind. 'I did want it all at one time. You know, the wife and kids and the white picket fence. After my parents died all I wanted was to re-create that feeling of having my family around me.'

'And now? That's what's available to you but you're pushing us all away.' Izzy was tired of paying for someone else's mistakes. She and the babies deserved more than that.

'At first I was afraid you regretted our night together, that there was no real future for us. I tried to fight those feelings I had for you, which were about more than getting you back into bed again.' He grinned at her and she didn't know what had shaken her more, that smile, him opening up to her, or finally telling her he thought about her as more than a convenience. Whatever it was, she wanted more of it.

'I thought I could separate our relationship from the babies. A stupid notion, I know, but in my head, loving them could be my ultimate downfall. You never gave me any indication you wanted anything serious between us and I thought if you decided someday you could do better than me, I'd lose these babies the same way I lost the last one.' That pain was still so obvious in his eyes and in his quivering voice Izzy could understand why he was still trying to protect himself, even if it came at the price of her peace of mind.

'These are your babies too. I would never take them away from you. A family means more to me than anything because, unlike you, I've never had one, Cal. You don't know what it's like to grow up knowing your own parents didn't want you and people had to be paid to take you in. I've had so many foster parents I don't remember all of their names. I want better for my children. I need them to know they're loved every day of their lives. That means growing up in a house with a father who shows them that and, let's be honest, you haven't been thrilled at the prospect of becoming a dad, have you?'

If they were sweeping away the debris from the past to clear the path for a happy future together then they needed to be completely honest with each other.

'I've told you why I've been holding back. I'm sorry I can't give you more than that.' He was leaving it up to her to decide if she was willing to risk her heart again on a future with someone who couldn't commit one hundred per cent to her.

'I appreciate your honesty, but I need someone who's going to put me first, to make my children his priority. It might seem selfish, but after Gerry I'm done with being second best.' There was every chance Cal could tell her to get lost with her demands, but it was better to know now if she was asking too much from him than finding out when it was too late.

'Hey, I'm not Gerry.' He sounded angry at the comparison and it was no wonder after everything he'd heard about his predecessor, but this wasn't about soothing his ego. It was about protecting her babies.

'Was everything okay for you?' Their waiter with the bad sense of timing arrived back at the table, staring pointedly at the discarded plates still laden with food.

'Fine, thanks.' Izzy didn't mean to snap but she wanted to finish this conversation before Cal shut her out again and left her guessing about where they stood as a couple or as a family.

Suitably cowed, he cleared the table without further comment. Cal waited until he was completely out of earshot before he continued his defence.

'Gerry was selfish, not thinking of anyone but himself in the decisions he made. I like to think I'm doing the opposite. I want to take my time and make sure everything I'm doing is for the right reasons. I won't apologise for wanting to do right by all of us.' With that logic Izzy couldn't fault him.

Perhaps it was a lot to expect him to outline all his plans for the future, including how he was going to feel about the babies once they got here, when it was clear he was still trying to adjust to the idea of being a father.

Cal got up to pay the bill, not waiting for it to be brought to the table, and Izzy had to hurry to catch him as he exited the restaurant without her. He was angry at having to justify himself to her yet again and she realised she had to make some concessions for the way he had let her stay with him in the first place, despite his reservations.

'Cal, stop. Please.' This evening could've been a chance for a romantic evening together, strengthening that connection she so desperately wanted. Instead she was in danger of pushing him away for ever by asking so much of him.

'It's just… I don't know what I'd do without you, Cal. I'm afraid of losing you.' Standing there in the street, with Cal refusing to even look at her, was sufficient to make her teary. She'd done the unthinkable and fallen for him somewhere along the way. It wasn't simply that she'd become accustomed to him being there for her, providing for her every need, but he'd become part of her life, part of her. Without him she knew she couldn't function properly and that wasn't a position she'd ever intended to let herself get into again when it meant depending on one person for her happiness.

He came back to her in a heartbeat, sliding his hands around her waist and rubbing his nose against hers. 'I'm not going anywhere without you, Fizz, unless you ask me to.'

It wasn't a declaration of undying love, but she was sure it was there in his kiss as he claimed her mouth once more. He was tender and loving, as he was in all things, but Izzy demanded proof this time that this was more than him simply comforting or placating her.

She weaved her fingers into his mop of unruly hair and pulled him in deeper, seeking to find if the true nature of his affections transcended mere emotions. There was no mistaking the extent of his loyalty to her but she didn't want either of them to confuse it for something else that might never have been there in the first place.

She needn't have worried. Once she gave

the green light that this was what she wanted from him, Cal pulled her hard against him, his passion leaving her legs weak at the knees.

Her skin prickled with awareness and the hairs on the back of her neck stood to attention as he showered her with kiss after kiss. He sought her with his bold tongue and teased her with little licks and flicks until she was grinding against him with longing.

Eventually they remembered to breathe, and she was glad to find she wasn't the only one panting after the unexpected encounter.

'We should probably go home,' he said half-heartedly, making no attempt to release her from his grasp.

'Mmm.'

Izzy was happy where she was but excited about moving their relationship forward. Cal had been as straightforward as he could be with her and it was up to her to decide if that was enough to base her future on. She had to ask herself if he was worth the gamble with her heart when there was no guarantee it was all going to work out this time either. Despite her whole body screaming, *Yes!*

CHAPTER NINE

THE JOURNEY HOME had given Cal some time to cool his ardour and think about more than what his libido was demanding. Izzy had told him in no uncertain terms what having a family meant to her, but he wasn't completely sure he felt the same as he once had about the idea. It wasn't fair to bed her and give her false hope that they were going to live happily ever after.

She deserved a partner who was totally committed to her and the babies, with no doubts about what he wanted. Until he found that certainty for himself he thought it best to cool things down between them again.

When they got back to the house he left her at the bottom of the stairs with, 'Goodnight, Izzy.'

This time his mouth barely grazed her

cheek as he kissed her before going to bed. Alone. He hoped she understood he wasn't rejecting her on a personal level but taking precautions for both of their sakes.

There was a very real chance they'd both be lying awake tonight on either side of the wall separating their bedrooms, replaying the passion they'd given in to completely. He'd been doing that anyway since the very first time he'd laid his lips on her.

So much for taking a step back and focusing on being a support to Izzy rather than being further cause for stress. She was vulnerable after her scare and didn't need him making a move on her when her hormones and emotions were all over the place. As were his. Especially since she'd kissed him back, her eyes and her body asking him for more.

Cal groaned, lifted the book he'd been reading from his nightstand in deference to the sleep that had been eluding him recently.

He managed a page or two before he realised not a single word had registered He was listening out for the sound of Izzy coming upstairs to bed.

'This is insane,' he confided to the fluffy

sheep Izzy had made him keep on his bed. It was impossible to concentrate on anything but the creak of the floorboards as she crossed to her room and the thought of her getting undressed for bed. Despite only wearing his boxers, Cal was beginning to sweat.

He tossed the book back onto his nightstand, not even bothering to mark his place, and turned the bedside light off. Eyes closed, he tried to force himself into slumber, knowing tomorrow at work would be as physically demanding as ever. Gone were the nights when he'd slept fitfully on the sofa because his bed held such painful connotations of the woman who'd broken his heart. Only for them to be replaced with lustful thoughts of the woman who'd been right by his side for years.

In the too-quiet darkness he thought he could hear her tossing and turning on her mattress. If he was being kept awake by thoughts of how that bubbling chemistry between them was threatening to explode again, perhaps she was too. Or, as he'd predicted all along, was she too confused after

Gerry's death and their twin surprise she didn't know what she was doing?

'Cal?' Suddenly Izzy's soft voice called to him in the darkness. At first he thought he'd imagined it, then he heard her footsteps cross his floor. He'd been so lost in his own head he hadn't realised she'd left her own room.

'Izzy? What's wrong?' By the time he managed to turn the bedside lamp on again she was sitting on the bed beside him. His brain was working overtime, trying to figure out what could possibly be wrong with her when she looked so calm. If there had been an issue with the babies she would've been in full panic mode by now.

Instead, she curled up in the foetal position beside him so their heads were side by side on his pillows. 'I don't want to sleep alone, Cal.'

She didn't appear to be in a hurry to go anywhere so he snuggled down beside her and pulled the covers over them. His heart was beating just as fast as it had when they'd kissed but he was doing his best not to misinterpret her meaning.

He couldn't help but reach out and touch

her, brush the russet tresses off her shoulder to reveal the porcelain skin beneath.

'Are you sure you don't want to make the most of the peace while you've got it?' Cal tried to conceal his optimism that she was here for more than company with a lame attempt at humour. However, when she rested a hand possessively on his hip, the lower half of his body jerked wide awake.

'Don't make me beg, Cal. You know neither of us would venture into this lightly, but we don't seem to be able to stop it happening either. I don't want to stop it.'

Lying in his own bed, with Izzy saying everything he wanted to hear, touching him with confidence that he was hers, Cal was completely undone.

Izzy was putting everything on the line by being here. By climbing into Cal's bed, not only was she risking further rejection but if he kicked her out now the last of her dignity would slink out the door with her.

An evening unsuccessfully dodging the sexual tension arcing between them, on top of the close relationship they already had, had been sufficient for her to act on. She knew he'd turned away from her tonight because he didn't want her to read more into his actions than he was offering.

For now, she'd be happy for him to acknowledge the attraction with more than a passionate kiss. It wasn't in her nature to throw herself at a man, but she knew Cal better than most. He wouldn't take advantage of her, quite the opposite. It wasn't difficult to tell he'd been holding back for her sake. If there was one thing preventing them from moving their relationship on to the next level it was liable to be because he was afraid of her getting hurt somewhere along the way. He'd already voiced his fears to that effect but as far as she could see it was too late, the kisses they'd shared were proof they were powerless to stop this runaway train anyway.

She ran her hand down his corded thigh, his skin hot enough beneath her fingertips for her to suggest he take off the last of his clothes.

His mouth kicked up at the corners, his eyes darkened and then his mouth was on hers, no longer constrained by concerns for her welfare.

Unleashed by his conscience, it seemed

Cal was as eager to explore this evolving dynamic as Izzy. He took command of her lips, moulding them to fit his. His hand was in her hair, drawing her closer, unashamed to let her know how his body was responding to her touch.

With her eyes closed, giving herself over to the sensation of his hands and lips sweeping over her, she was already drifting away on a cloud of pleasure. Only the pure need for him she experienced when he slipped the strap of her night dress down her shoulder and cupped her naked breast grounded her again.

He brushed his thumb lightly over her nipple and she jerked back into her body with the sudden rush of arousal in response. Her reaction to that brief, intimate contact spurred him on to extract more of it from her. Cal moved his hungry mouth from hers, sucking and tasting her skin as he moved to her neck, her collarbone, and—*oh, yes*—her breast.

She sucked in a shaky breath of arousal as he slid the other strap down to follow its neighbour and flicked her nipple with the tip of his tongue. Izzy clutched his shoulders, arched her body further against his and demanded more. The first swell of ecstasy began to build inside her once he drew the responsive nub into his mouth. She'd forgotten how good it was to simply let herself go, enjoying the moment with him.

Cal grazed his teeth over her sensitive skin and sucked hard, ripping a cry of pure ecstasy from deep inside her very core. This time she didn't even waste time on the niceties of inviting him to undress, letting her hands do the work until he was fully naked beneath her fingertips. He did the same for her, sliding the rest of her nightdress excruciatingly slowly down her body and kissing every newly exposed inch of her skin until she was completely naked, and he was kneeling at her feet.

'You're beautiful,' he said, and though she felt a little bashful, with nowhere to hide her blossoming body under the glare of the bedside light, Cal's obvious appreciation was there for her to see.

'So are you.' She repaid the compliment with as much sincerity as it had been given to her. The nature of their relationship in the past, and up until recently, meant she'd tried not to recall what he looked like out of the padded flight suit. Now she was free to let her eyes feast once more on his impressive, solid physique and the majesty of his arousal.

Cal's smile was so big it crinkled the skin at the corners of his eyes and made him even more devilishly delicious as he covered her body with his. Her limbs were trembling with anticipation she wanted him so badly. With him nibbling the skin at her neck, his erection intimately teasing her, she was on the edge of flipping him over onto his back and climbing on top of him. Just when she thought his restraint was proving greater than hers he nudged her thighs apart and groaned a satisfied 'Oh...' as he entered her.

It was a moment of perfect joy and peace for her as they were finally joined together in body as well as soul. He paused, his eyes searching her face, and she could tell he was waiting for confirmation she was okay. She didn't want her condition or his fierce desire to protect her at all costs to inhibit this pivotal, much-longed-for moment in their partnership. They had to learn to trust each other's instincts as well as their own if they were going to have a future together.

'I need you, Cal.' She needed all of him with no holding back because she wanted to give him everything of herself in return.

Her plea, her surrender freed them both from the last threads of restraint and let them search together for that ultimate pleasure goal.

'My Isobel…' His husky voice in her ear, the sweet affectation and the delicious fullness of having him inside her was too much for her to bear. She was at breaking point, desperately clinging on to prolong this feeling of ecstasy as long as possible.

With every grind of his hips, every thrust and using every trick he had in his locker to drive her wild, he made her cries more frequent, higher pitched until she was sure she'd shatter every window in the house.

Then the world was spinning somewhere far below her as she soared with one last push from her equally vocal partner.

They clung together for as long as their limbs held out, panting and grinning at each other like loons.

Izzy was so elated, if it wasn't for the obvious, one would've been forgiven for thinking this was her first time and she'd given herself to her first love. She'd had good sex before, and with him, but they were looking at each other with a certain smugness that said they'd both achieved a new level together.

'Why didn't we want to do this again?' Cal asked as he lay down beside her, still caressing her naked body and sending aftershocks of her climax rippling through her again and again.

'I think we were worried we'd burn each other out.' To illustrate the point that they'd have trouble keeping their hands off each other, she cupped his backside and squeezed.

The truth, they both knew, was much more complicated and painful than that. Although she couldn't speak for him, Izzy couldn't regret that time when it had given her so much to look forward to now and had brought her and Cal closer than they'd ever been.

'Hmm, I hope this isn't simply your way of guaranteeing the babies get a room each.'

It didn't escape her notice he was avoiding talking seriously about their future as a couple but as long as he continued to think of this as a permanent arrangement they were good.

As for Izzy, she knew she was in love with

him and their epic lovemaking had confirmed it. Hopefully in time he'd come to feel the same, but it was too much to ask for now when the wounds Janet had inflicted were still raw. It was different for her when she and Gerry had had definitive closure. The same couldn't be said for Janet, who'd made her presence known so recently it still pained Izzy to think about it. With no discernible conscience about what she'd done, Izzy wouldn't put it past her to keep turning up like the proverbial bad penny.

That left a smidgen of doubt that Cal would remain committed to her should Janet decide she preferred his attentions and wanted him back. They had a long history together, Janet had been someone Cal had imagined having a family with, and that wasn't a thought easily dismissed. She, though, was always getting carried away on dreams of the family they could make once the twins were born.

'Just wait until I try to talk you into installing a swimming pool.' This wasn't the time for deep and meaningful conversations or displays of jealousy and insecurity. She wanted to keep things fun and flirty, not to mention irresistible, so he'd come back for more. 'I won't let you get out of bed until you agree to my every demand.'

'Do your worst,' he said, lying spread-eagled on the bed, his body ready to be persuaded by anything she said or did.

Always keen to show she was every bit as physically capable as the next person, Izzy rose to the challenge and took charge.

'Are you ready to go?' Izzy peeped her head around the bedroom door, but Cal simply pulled the covers back up over his head.

'No.'

She chuckled and plonked herself down on the bed beside him. 'You can't stay in there all day.'

'Why not? It sounds like a good idea to me.'

Izzy shrieked as he reached for her and tried to pull her under the covers with him. It was very tempting to climb back in with him when his bedhead hair and morning stubble made him look even more handsome than usual.

Now they knew how phenomenal they were together in all aspects of their relationship she could happily spend the day here with him making up for lost time. She'd heard an increased libido could happen at any stage of pregnancy, but she reckoned he'd have had this effect on her every time he touched her, long after her body was her own again.

'I. Would. Love. To,' she said, through his kisses along her collarbone, and he palmed her breast through her blouse to illustrate how keen he was for her to get naked with him again. 'But we have an appointment to get to.'

'We do?'

It wasn't fair to tease her like this, awakening that ache for him inside her when they couldn't do anything about it.

'I booked us into a practical parenting class.'

'Isn't it a little early for that? I thought antenatal classes were for much later in pregnancy.' Cal frowned and seemed to withdraw to the far side of the bed. Obviously, they still had some work to do when it came to his role as a hands-on dad.

'True, but this isn't any ordinary class. It's a private course focused on parenting twins, and I hear it's very popular, so it books up

early. I thought we could both use some tips.'
She wanted them to be the best parents they
could be for the children.

'I'll need all the help I can get,' he muttered as he pulled the duvet away.

'Cal? Are you sure you want to be my
birthing partner? I don't want to force you
into it if you really don't want to be there.'
There was only so much she could do if he
genuinely didn't want to be involved.

She wanted nothing more than to have
him coaching her through her contractions
as their babies were delivered into the world.
Although they both had baggage they were
dealing with, these babies represented their
future together. She wouldn't have asked him
to be part of the birth if she wasn't thinking
of him as her real-life partner and the family
they were going to make together.

Cal took both her hands in his and looked
her deep in the eyes. 'It would be a privilege
to be there for you.'

If Izzy could only believe his devotion extended to the little people they'd created together, everything would be just perfect.

CHAPTER TEN

'HI, EVERYONE. I'M SHARON. Help yourselves to tea and biscuits and make yourselves comfortable.' The woman holding the practical parenting class directed the anxious-looking couples huddled by the door towards the refreshments table.

Cal poured out two cups of tea and watched Izzy load a plate with enough chocolate biscuits to see them through the whole day. At last she was heeding the snacking advice. With any luck they'd get through this class without any fainting incidents. He hadn't been thrilled by the idea of coming here today but he supposed it would be useful to pick up some practical tips today on living with twins.

Janet hadn't even wanted him to attend the scans with her and she'd probably had Dar-

ren accompany her to the antenatal classes
when the time had come. It no longer bothered him. He was just grateful Izzy was
making such an effort to get him involved
and feel part of this pregnancy.

They were embarking on an exciting new
chapter of their lives, not only as a couple
but they were about to be thrown into the
deep end with the arrival of the twins too.
Izzy had accepted him as her partner and
that was enough for him. It meant he could
be here to support her when she didn't have
any family around to help. Cal hoped that
through these classes he'd see exactly what
he could do to make life easier for her. Even
if it was just being there to mop her brow
or have his fingers crushed during labour. It
was better for Izzy's well-being to know she
had someone who'd be by her side through-
out this journey.

He glanced around the room at the other
couples. There were married pairs, mothers
and daughters and best friends. Every couple was different, but the common theme
was that loving bond like the one he had
with Izzy. It would've been tough for Izzy to
have come here on her own and tougher for

him if he had missed out. Some things a person could never get back and thankfully he'd realised that before he'd missed out on any more of their babies' important milestones.

The presentation began with a talk on what made multiple birth pregnancies different from single pregnancies. A lot of which he and Izzy were already aware of due to their medical experience but hearing there was a higher risk of complications and need for more health professionals at the birth was different when you were preparing for real.

There were plenty of helpful tips for them to take some of the stress out of coping with more than one baby. Including bathtimes and having all necessary supplies at hand before attempting to bath the babies, one at a time. A lot of the general advice was focused on support and making sure there was more than one pair of hands available when possible. Something he intended to do. In fact, he was looking forward to sharing the bathing and feeding with Izzy and forging a bond with their babies.

They were given a couple of dolls to practise changing nappies on and Sharon came to supervise their attempts.

'I can see Dad has done this before. Well done.'

There was a good reason he had his baby doll changed in seconds whilst Izzy was still grappling with the tapes on her twin's nappy. He'd had a lot of experience when his nephews and nieces had been young. Back then, when they'd all come together at his parents' house for special occasions, he'd made the most of his precious uncle time. As far as he'd been concerned, it was practice for the family he'd always expected to have, and his sisters had been over the moon when he'd volunteered for changing duty.

This practical lesson should have been overwhelming to someone who'd been doing his best not to get too involved beyond providing practical support, but it reminded him of the joy he'd once experienced being around children. Before life with Janet had attached negative connotations with the idea of being a father. Now he and Izzy were making moves towards being a real couple it was about time he stopped catastrophising, imagining the worst outcome, and enjoyed every moment life together would bring them.

He looked around at the other couples all mucking in together to change their pretend babies whilst he was standing back watching Izzy struggle do it alone.

'Let me help, Iz. We're a team, remember?' She gave him a wary look, and he knew it was going to take time to convince her he meant every word, but he had months left to prove himself. He was going to be the best father Izzy could ever wish to have for her children.

As they arrived back at the car after the class Cal caught sight of a couple exiting the maternity wing with their newborn in one of those carriers he'd had to buy for the twins. The pair were obviously new parents, that glow of unconditional love for the life they'd just created lighting them up like Christmas trees. Cal smiled, anticipating the day he and Izzy would experience walking out that door as first-time parents too.

The little family stepped out into the sunshine and it was then everything hit home. These weren't just random strangers he was watching start a new chapter of their lives together, it was Janet and Darren and the baby he'd been father to for its first weeks of existence.

They were oblivious to anyone's presence, in their little bubble of pure joy, and it was like a kick in the gut for Cal. Not because he was jealous of Darren but because he'd never seen Janet look so at peace. Leaving him had obviously been the best thing she could have done. He would never have made her this happy. Blinded by his desire for a family at any cost, he hadn't seen the flaws in their relationship at the time, but it was obvious now he'd never loved her the way he loved Izzy.

They'd never had the same connection or interests and, looking back, something had always been lacking in their relationship. It must have been for Janet to go looking for more with another man and for Cal to be happy for them walking away as a family. Izzy was the best thing to have ever happened to him and this encounter proved it.

'Is everything all right?' Izzy was sitting in the car, waiting for Cal to get in. His attention was elsewhere, and it hadn't taken long for her to figure out why. Janet was like a dead weight around her neck, dragging her down every time she thought she was making progress with Cal.

'Fine.' He got in and closed the door, making no mention of the scene across the road. If it didn't bother him he would've referenced the couple exiting the hospital with their new bundle of joy but clearly it was still hurting that he was no longer part of it.

It was difficult not to take that personally and have it pierce her heart until it felt as though her life blood was draining slowly and painfully away every time she thought of the longing on his face. He wanted his ex and her baby over Izzy and his own children. That was the family he was supposed to have, and they were simply the imposters he'd been landed with.

It wasn't fair to carry on pretending this was going to work out when she'd been forcing him into this relationship every step of the way. Perhaps she'd been trying to convince herself he only needed time to learn to love her and the babies because deep down she was afraid of doing this alone. She'd been out of her depth in that class even with their fake twins whilst Cal had been the calm, capable one. It was in that moment, holding that doll, not even knowing how to change a nappy properly, that it had hit home what a huge undertaking motherhood was going to be for her. There were going to be two precious mites totally dependent on her to protect and provide for them as well as guide them through life. Difficult to do when she hadn't had any role models who'd done the same for her. What if she couldn't handle it like all of those who were supposed to have parented her?

She didn't want to have children who resented her and rejected a relationship with her once they were old enough to leave home. Although she hadn't realised it, she'd been acting the role of parent as much as Cal. If they carried on pretending they knew what they were getting into they were going to end up resenting each other for getting trapped in a situation that would be much harder to get out of once the twins arrived.

They'd be taking a huge gamble on the future if they stayed together and she wasn't prepared to do that again. Cal deserved that same level of happiness he'd witnessed in Janet and she wasn't convinced she could give him that. Izzy didn't want either of them settling for second best.

So much for putting her mind at ease. Regardless of the information leaflets she had tucked in her bag and all the stress-relieving tips they'd been given, Izzy was more wound up than ever by the time they got home.

She'd been so caught up in that idea of her happy family coming together that she'd only today realised something capable of bringing her back down to earth with a thump. No amount of cajoling was going to make Cal love these babies.

Her crush and her bond with Cal had, on her part at least, evolved into real love. She was grateful to him for providing a roof for her and she wanted him to be part of her babies' lives but not if he didn't love these babies the way she loved them.

'Have you taken your supplements today?' It was a simple enough question but now when she was analysing every conversation Cal's focus on the pregnancy only ever seemed to centre around her health. His interest seemed limited to that of a doctor rather than a prospective father.

'Yes. You don't have to keep reminding me.' Now she was becoming vexed on behalf of her unborn children, memories of her own childhood made her snappy with him.

Those big eyes full of hurt at her tone might have made her feel as though she'd just kicked a puppy, but she'd fallen for that guilt trick too many times with Gerry. Time and again she'd been promised a life of her dreams only to find it was nothing more than an illusion. Foster families, her parents, even Gerry had conned her into thinking she'd found security, only to snatch it away again when they discovered life with her lacking in some way.

The circumstances might be different with Cal but they were also scarily similar. Despite promises to herself not to get too invested in a relationship again, or rely on any one person solely for support, she'd left her home and jumped into bed with him. If he didn't want this family as much as she did, wasn't completely and madly in love with all three of them, then her future was as rocky as ever.

With sleepless nights and double the mess a newborn usually brought, Cal would tire quickly of them all invading his space. Izzy wasn't prepared to expose her children to the same uncertainty she'd grown up in.

'What's wrong? Please don't feel too over-whelmed by it all. We can go through those information leaflets together later and work on your birth plan if you like.'

'As a matter of fact, I have been thinking about the birth. I'm wondering if it's a good idea for you to be there after all.' It hurt to say it, even more to see him flinch as though she'd punched him in the gut. But theirs was a complicated relationship created mostly through circumstances. They needed some way to separate those feelings encompass-ing friendship, love and loyalty.

'I thought we'd already discussed this?'

After a brief lapse Izzy's barriers were back up, protecting her, and she needed the truth, not some fantastic version of it, be-fore she'd let him bypass them again. In the long run, telling her only what he thought she wanted to hear now would cause greater distress later when it turned out not to be true. Her heart bore the scars of experience.

'Do you want these babies, or just me?' Cal had never made a declaration of love to her, never mind the babies, and it should be a requirement for a man who expected to be in their lives.

'Can't I have both?' He genuinely didn't appear to understand her concerns but that was half of the problem. If he had that nursery filled and someone in his bed, he'd be content to coast along. Whereas she wasn't prepared to let her family merely exist.

'You've done so much, Cal, but I worry you only want us to replace everything Janet took from you. I'm not getting any real emotional connection between you and the babies.' It was harsh, but she needed to figure out his true intentions. If this wasn't going to work out she'd have to make alternative accommodation arrangements and time was running out before the twins arrived. Izzy couldn't bring them back from the hospital to a house that was full of tension because she was afraid to trust the man they were supposed to live with.

He was pacing the room, hands on his hips, nostrils flaring—all the symptoms of someone trying not to lose their cool. Hardly surprising, she supposed, when it would seem as though she was turning on him after all he'd done for her. She should be jumping at the chance of having someone like that in her life but the string of liars she'd endured over the years had left her suspicious, even of a good man like Cal.

'You really think that of me? That I would offer you everything I had, make love to you, provide a home for you and our babies, all so I could pick up where I left off with a woman who'd clearly never loved me?' His gasp of disbelief did make her falter in her assumptions. He made it, her, sound crazy, but she'd been able to twist all his good intentions to fit some darker purpose because it suited her better than risking her heart again.

Izzy threw her hands up. 'I don't know any more.'

'You don't know any more...' His mumbling was punctuated with soulless laughter as he scrubbed his hands through his hair. The display of frustration at her lack of faith in him was as effective as if he'd burst into tears and she hated herself for putting him through this necessary test of his devotion.

'Don't get cross with me, Cal. Everything's just so...confusing.' Her head was beginning to hurt with all the back and forth going on in there. Everything in her heart wanted to believe they were going to have their happy ending but her head knew better and was working overtime to remind her of everything that could potentially go wrong.

He stopped pacing like a caged bear and came to stand in front of her, resting his hands on her shoulders and imploring her to look him in the eye. 'Why? I've been honest with you from the start about only wanting to do right by you. I never expected to fall in love with you. I know it's complicated things, but I thought we'd be able to work things out.'

He loved her, and she wished that was all she'd needed to hear from him. Wished that it made every misgiving she had about their future flap its wings and take flight.

'I'm sorry but it's not enough for me.'

'What have I done wrong?' In truth he'd been the perfect partner in every way imaginable. It was his potential as a father that made her wary of continuing their relationship if his heart lay elsewhere. The babies were never going to be good enough for him, just as she'd never been good enough for anyone in her life.

'Family is everything to me, Cal, but we both know this one doesn't include you.'

'I can only give you what I can but if it's not enough…' He faltered then, his hands falling from her shoulders as he let his true pain at the situation show. She'd been so selfish, thinking only of how she was affected by these great life-changing moments. Cal was every bit as insecure and damaged by his past as she was.

Izzy suddenly realised he was right, she was the one in the wrong here. He'd been bending over backwards to make her life easier, to make her feel wanted, and all this time she'd been looking for excuses as to why things couldn't work between them.

'I know. I'm so sorry.' It was a mess and all she'd done was destroy a relationship that could have stood a chance.

Izzy tried to reach out to him and he physically shrank away from her touch as though he couldn't bear her to touch him. She wanted to vomit.

'I told you everything Janet had put me through, you don't think that was humili-ating enough for me?' It had taken him so long to open up to her again, Izzy knew how hurt and embarrassed he'd been by Janet's betrayal.

Arms folded, lips drawn into a thin line, his body seemed to close in on itself as he physically and emotionally withdrew from her, and Izzy realised she was about to lose everything.

'You saved me, Cal, and now I don't know what I, what we, would do without you.' The babies kicked her as though to remind her she was coming close to stuffing things up for all of them. In trying to protect herself from a man who'd never put her first, she'd lost sight of the man who always did.

Cal couldn't keep track of the emotional roller-coaster he'd been strapped into since last night when Izzy had climbed into his bed. He'd been delighted to jump on board then for the ride of his life. With her in his arms all night he'd believed it was the start of their rest of their life together. Now? It was like finding that note pinned to the fridge all over again.

'Yeah. I'm always good for picking up the pieces of the mess other men have left behind.' Janet had used him as some sort of back-up when Darren hadn't immediately stepped forward to be the father of her baby. She'd taken advantage of his desire to be part of a family again and milked him for everything he was worth in terms of money, love and attention. He'd never expected Izzy to do the same.

When someone, or something, better came along, she'd dump him quicker than a dirty nappy. It was his fault for getting into exactly the same situation again after vowing never to let any woman play him the way Janet had done. This was worse. Izzy had been his friend and confidante long before he'd fallen in love with her. Another one-sided love affair doomed to end in heartache for him.

After Janet, he hadn't thought he had anything left to lose. Now he was back in that same position with his heart, his home and his future on the line, and he had to take back some control. In another few months the babies would be here and there would be no going back.

'At the minute I feel as though I've been drafted in as a last-minute substitute to save the day, rather than someone you'd planned to be with for the rest of your life.' He was too angry, too hurt to hold back and save her feelings. He'd been doing that for too long with too many people and it was about time he was able to say what he really thought. Except getting it off his chest was doing nothing to make this any easier.

'To be fair, neither of us had planned for this to happen, Cal, and I'm sorry if you think I somehow tricked my way into your affections. If you knew me the way I thought you did, you'd realise I'm not that devious.'

'I'm beginning to think I don't know you at all.'

'So, what are you saying? That you want to put an end to this now? Do you want me to move out?' With her arms folded Izzy challenged him directly, instead of skirting around the problem the way he and Janet obviously had. If he'd known then what the problem between them had been, he wouldn't have hesitated in ending their relationship himself, but this situation with Izzy wasn't so clear cut.

He didn't want to act in the heat of the moment in case he'd come to regret it. 'I need some time to think things through.'

'I—I'll pack a bag.' Izzy didn't argue, cry, shout or do anything to show she had any passion about what they did next and that made Cal question the whole nature of their relationship when his heart was breaking. He didn't want to split now with no way back until he had some space away from the situation to see it from a different perspective, but he wasn't sure Izzy was of the same opinion.

'No, I'll go.'

He wouldn't ask her to move out unless he was one hundred per cent sure that was what they both thought was for the best. With children involved they couldn't be that sort of couple who split and got back together whenever the mood took them. Stability was the keyword in a child's life and in that of a man who'd been burned once too many times.

'No matter what you think of me, I wouldn't ask you to move out of your own house.'

'You're not. It's my decision.' It was the

last vestige of control he apparently had in this relationship. This time, if things were ending he wanted it to be on his terms.

CHAPTER ELEVEN

WHEN CAL HAD LEFT, Izzy had thought she'd never stop crying. Somehow she'd managed to throw away her one chance of a real family. Her own damn insecurities and inability to trust had caused him to cast her in the same mould as Janet. She couldn't blame him when he'd given her everything and all she'd done was take. The irony was that the second he walked out the door she knew exactly what she wanted. Cal. The babies. A family.

The only ember of hope she had left that that could still be a possibility was that he hadn't thrown her out on the street. It was typical of Cal to let her stay in his house and make himself temporarily homeless, even when he was mad at her. She didn't know why she'd ever doubted his integrity. Oh, wait, it probably had something to do with a series of unreliable guardians and one flaky boyfriend. Things that had absolutely nothing to do with Cal and everything to do with her personal baggage.

It had been days now since he'd walked out, and she felt every second of it. She'd grieved more over losing Cal than she had for Gerry. Which highlighted the differences between the two relationships and the two men involved. Not to mention the strength of the love in her heart for one over the other.

The relief and renewed sense of purpose she'd expected on her return to work had been overshadowed by the sadness at seeing Cal there, not being able to touch him or tell him how much she loved him. She didn't even know where he'd been staying because he hadn't stopped long enough to utter more than two words to her. He could barely look at her and she didn't know what she could do to fix everything she'd broken.

Every time she tried to initiate a conversation he'd simply say, 'Not here, not now,' and expect her to back off without complaint, and she had done until now.

They couldn't carry on avoiding each

other for ever. She cornered him in the staff-room, which he had a habit of retreating into so he could avoid her in the radio room. One of her dagger looks in the direction of the other crew members he was using as cover and they scurried off, knowing where they weren't wanted.

Izzy stood in the doorway, blocking Cal's escape route, so he had no choice but to acknowledge her or attempt to push past her, and he was too much of a gentleman to do that.

'Cal, please talk to me. Shout at me, tell me to get out of your house or kiss me sense-less and tell me we can work this out. Anything has to be better than this limbo we're in.' Okay, that last one was more of a fantasy than an option, but she'd spent these last days running through every scenario and that was the one she preferred.

'This isn't—'

'Don't tell me this isn't the time or the place when you haven't given me any choice. You can't stay away from your own house indefinitely and we can't go on ignoring each other at work. It's killing me.' It wasn't fair to leave her wondering if they still had a chance if he'd already made his mind up it was over. If they couldn't resolve the issues she'd caused she'd have to do something drastic, like leave her job rather than seeing him every day and realising what she'd thrown away. With the babies coming, job security wasn't something she took lightly but there was no way she could carry on here with a reminder of everything she'd lost staring her in the face every day.

'You don't think those things you said to me didn't almost destroy me? I don't think it's too much to ask for a little time out when you accused me of being some sort of conman simply because I loved you?'

He tossed the newspaper he'd been reading onto the chair as he got to his feet and slammed his coffee cup on the table, sloshing the contents everywhere. Cal had every reason to be angry and Izzy was almost grateful to see this blazing fire in his eyes that said all might not be lost after all. He'd said he'd loved her and that wasn't something a person could turn on and off at will. Whilst she was still able to rouse such a passionate display of emotion in him there was hope he hadn't stopped loving her altogether.

'I was scared, Cal, afraid history was going to repeat itself. That my dream of my little family was going to be taken from me again.' Her voice was cracking with the threat of tears, not at the memory of how people had treated her in the past but because she'd got it so wrong this time. She'd let the past steal away the one person who had actually loved her.

Cal took a step forward and for a moment she almost believed he was going to take her into his arms and tell her everything would be all right. Then the alarm rang out for all standby crew to head to the hangar and any notion of a reconciliation vanished.

'I have to go.'

There was never any doubt a call would take priority over Izzy, but she didn't want to let him go without some assurance that they'd made some progress today after she'd opened her heart to him. 'But you'll come and see me when you get back, yes?'

He looked as though he was about to refuse her, and she had to swallow the ball of disappointment lodged in her throat. Then he gave a quick nod before disappearing out the door.

That one spark of hope that she could salvage her relationship with Cal, along with the future for her and her children she'd been afraid was too good to be true, let her breathe again. Suddenly all that pent-up tension and worry ebbed away, taking with it what little energy she had and leaving her doubled over like a ragdoll.

Pain zipped across her belly, along with the feeling of being caught in a vice. Contractions weren't to be expected at this stage, it was too early. She tried to call out for Cal, but another sharp pain stole her breath away. Tears blurred her vision as she staggered over to grip the chair he'd vacated only moments earlier. Another spike of agony and with it a trickle of fluid running down the inside of her leg. Her waters had broken.

This was everything she'd feared come true. The twins wouldn't survive being born now and she was frightened and alone. She needed Cal.

'Isobel Fitzpatrick. Where is she?' Cal knew he'd probably broken all kind of rules in his desperate hurry to get to the hospital, but he didn't care about anything other than getting to Izzy.

'Are you her partner?' The woman at the desk didn't seem to understand the urgency of the matter as she kept tip-tapping away at the computer instead of immediately whisking him through to Izzy's bedside.

He leaned on the desk, trying not to act on the impulse to swipe everything on the floor. 'Yes. Her waters have broken.' *Get me to her now!*

Saying the words made his stomach roll again the way it had been doing since Mac had broken the news to him that she'd been taken to hospital. As soon as he'd heard that on his arrival back at base, he'd jumped to his car and high-tailed it to the hospital, cursing himself for not staying with her earlier. If he'd stayed to have that talk with her he would've been there for her. He would've been the one to get her the help she needed and comfort her when she would've been frightened about what was going to happen to the babies.

Then again, if he hadn't moved out in the first place he might've seen the signs something was wrong earlier, but he'd been too busy licking his wounds in a budget hotel for the past few days to notice. He hadn't even taken the time to check in with her at work to make sure she was eating properly and looking after herself because of his damn pride.

Yes, she'd questioned his commitment to their family, as he had done during his time out, but he hadn't stopped loving her. He wanted the best for her and the babies and should have prioritised their welfare over his bruised ego. Now the stress he'd put her through, thinking he was going to leave her, had probably caused her to miscarry, as the babies wouldn't be considered viable at this stage and there would be no medical intervention to strengthen their lungs. They were already so precious to him and Izzy. If it wasn't for those babies the two of them would never have realised how much they loved one another.

'Are you Cal?' A nurse at the desk seemed to take more interest in his arrival than the woman he was talking to.

'Yes. I'm looking for Isobel Fitzpatrick. I was told she'd been brought here.' If someone didn't take him to her soon he was going to do a loop of the corridors yelling her name until she answered him back.

'She's been asking for you. Come with me.' The nurse exchanged a few words with the receptionist before marching him down towards one of the wards.

The fact Izzy hadn't sent out an alert to the staff, banning him from the premises, was promising that she was willing to forgive him for walking out on her the way he had. Although that could change if the babies came early and suffered as a consequence. He would never forgive himself if the worst happened so he wouldn't blame her if she never wanted to see him again in those circumstances.

'How is she?' He was running after the nurse, begging for more information like any other anxious partner or father-to-be.

'Frightened, tearful, and stubbornly refusing to let these babies come early.' The half-smile gave him an idea of how hard Izzy was fighting to stay in control of this pregnancy.

Good.

'That's my Iz.' Those babies needed to hold on as long as possible. If they couldn't stop the labour the babies wouldn't survive, and it would be the same outcome if too much amniotic fluid had been lost. It was simply too early to do anything other than wait. There were so many things that could go wrong at this stage, but he knew everyone here would be keeping Izzy calm and comfortable until they had a clearer picture of what was going on.

'In here.' The nurse opened the door and led him into a side room where Izzy was lying on the bed. As soon as she saw him she burst into floods of tears as though she'd been holding them back all this time, waiting for him to come and be strong for her.

'Oh, Fizz, sweetheart.' He was on the verge of breaking down himself, seeing her lying there vulnerable and helpless and so unlike the woman he knew and loved.

'Cal? I'm so glad you're here...' She stretched her hand out toward him before lapsing into more sobs. He took the seat by the bed and smoothed her hair back from her forehead.

'Shh. It's all right. Everything's going to be okay.' It had to be.

'This is my fault. You told me I was over-doing it and I wouldn't listen. I'm just too damn stubborn for my own good and now we're going to lose the babies.'

'Now, if anyone's to blame, it's me. I shouldn't have left you on your own. I'm so sorry.' He kissed her forehead, refusing to let her feel guilty when he'd been the one who'd made her worry she might have to find somewhere else to live with their two children before they'd even been born. Now he'd happily hand over the keys to his house for ever if it would ease her mind and stop this nightmare.

'We've already talked about this, Isobel. This isn't anyone's fault. It happens. Now, the scan showed that both heartbeats are strong and though baby number two is surrounded by less amniotic fluid than baby number one, there's still plenty there. We'll keep an eye on that but hopefully, if there's no further leak and no sign of infection, we'll be able to send you home soon.' The midwife did her best to comfort them, but Cal knew that was a lot of ifs. The statistics weren't in their favour for survival when the amniotic sac had ruptured this early, but Izzy Fitzpatrick was much more than a statistic.

'Thank you.' He was grateful they'd been

here for Izzy when he hadn't, and luckily Mac had been the one to convince her to get to the hospital without delay. It meant they had every chance of getting the right outcome for Izzy and the babies.

'I'll leave her in your capable hands while I go and see about these test results and getting some antibiotics. Press this buzzer if you need any assistance in the meantime.' The attentive midwife unhooked the buzzer from behind the bed and left it on the bed for Izzy. It was a moment of privacy and a chance for a conversation he was no longer willing to avoid.

'Thank you for coming, Cal—'

'I'm so sorry for everything, Izzy—'

Their words tumbled over each other and he knew it was because of the seriousness of the situation. All the stuff that had caused the rift between them no longer mattered. They smiled at each other and she reached for his hand again.

'I thought I'd lost you.'

'Never. I was hurt but I meant it when I told you I'd never abandon you, Izzy. I love you. I don't care if you don't feel the same way about me, I just want to know you're all okay.' He was willing to put his feelings aside if that's what she wanted, if it meant he could remain in her life.

'Of course I love you, but I saw the way you looked at Janet with the baby. I thought you'd still rather be with them than us.'

He shook his head vigorously, unable to believe she could ever think that when everything he'd ever wanted was right here. 'Seeing them made me realise how lucky I was to have *you*. I never loved her the way I love you, Izzy. I can't wait to raise our family together.'

'Does this mean you'll move back home?' She was smiling now, those worry lines having faded away along with her tears.

'Is that what you want?' He daren't hope for anything beyond her health and happiness but it would be a relief if she genuinely wanted him with her after these past days convincing himself otherwise.

'Yes.' What Izzy wanted more than anything was to have her babies safely delivered at the right time and to go home, with Cal. She was grateful that Mac had been there at the base to make sure she'd got to hospital as soon as he had, but Cal was the only one she'd wanted.

Gone were the days when she'd expected to battle these difficult times alone. They were a team and if it hadn't been for their wobble after the parenting class he would never have moved out. She didn't want to go through any of this without him.

'Good.' He gave her an adorable half-smile that made her fall for him all over again. She knew she was in love with him, that was the reason she'd been so scared they weren't together for the right reasons. Now, having him here after everything she'd accused him of, she knew he was committed to this family. He'd told her he loved her, and this was the proof her twice-burned, baggage-carrying self had demanded before giving herself one hundred per cent to another man.

'I've missed you.' In case he didn't already know how much he meant to her, she was going to make sure to clarify things before they left this building. The time had passed for misunderstandings and skating around important issues. They needed to be a cohesive unit to face whatever the future held for them and the babies. Their babies.

'I've missed you too.' His voice cracked a little and he gave an embarrassed cough to clear his throat, but it was an emotional time for both of them. She could see he shared her worries about the twins and how close they'd come to losing everything.

'I'm sorry for questioning your motives for being with me. I guess I'm just wary of anyone who claims to love me but that's not your fault. You've done nothing but show me what true love is.' She'd pre-empted a disastrous relationship and almost willed it into existence because of her past experiences but all that had to change for the sake of her family. As long as Cal still thought she was worth the effort.

'I had a part to play in this whole mess too, thinking I could never make you truly happy and someday you'd walk out on me too. That's why I was afraid to let myself get close to the babies, thinking I'd never recover if you took them away from me. I guess it's too late for that anyway. The second I knew you were here I knew I loved you all, wanted to keep you all safe. I'm sorry it took so long for me to work it out, but I know my place is here, with you and the babies.'

That was everything she wanted to hear, and she could almost feel her body settling down to see out the rest of this pregnancy with him, free from further drama. 'Well, I'd prefer if we could do that doting partner thing at home.'

'You won't be allowed to lift a finger, you know. Do you think you can manage that?' His teasing came with a hint of genuine concern and it was little wonder when she'd been so difficult thus far, but she'd learned her lesson and hoped she'd get a second chance at this whole pampered pregnant lady thing. This time she'd take full advantage of everything Cal was offering.

'Complete bed rest. I swear.' She crossed her heart and promised to let him fuss over her. After these past days, wandering around that big house on her own, she didn't know why she'd resisted it this far. It was nice having someone worry about her and want to take care of her for once. A shame it had taken almost losing everything for her to appreciate that instead of fearing it.

'And after the babies are here? What happens then?' It was clear he was asking in terms of their relationship what would happen next, and though no one could predict the future she could be honest about her hopes for the future.

'I am hoping we live happily ever after. I love you, Cal, and I'm sure the babies will love you too. Can we think of this as our new start, our little family finally coming together?' It was something they'd both been missing out on and this pregnancy was a gift, giving them everything they'd dreamed about. With Cal in her corner she was optimistic they could persuade these babies to stay put until they were out of the danger zone.

A smile slowly crept over his face until he was positively beaming. 'You've never said that before.'

'What? That I love you? I think I was afraid to say it out loud and acknowledge those feelings myself. Now I've said it out loud, I can't take it back.' She gave a little laugh, still nervous about entering into another serious relationship, especially when there were going to be two more wee people affected by her every future decision, but leaping into the unknown with Cal was preferable to a lonely life without him.

'No, you can't, and I for one will never get sick of hearing you say it. Along with that "our family", thing you casually tossed in there. You don't know how happy that makes me, knowing that I'm going to be part of this.' He rested his hand on her bump and she couldn't imagine anyone else she would rather spend the rest of her life with, raising these precious babies. It was important he knew that because she didn't intend wasting any more of her life regretting things she did or didn't say.

'You're very much part of this, daddy Cal, and once we know for sure these two are going to behave and stay where they are until we're ready for them, I want to make it official. Calum Armstrong, will you marry us?' She hadn't known she was going to ask him until the words came out of her mouth, but it felt so right for all of them to make this relationship as solid as possible.

It was the first time she'd ever seen him lost for words as his jaw flopped open and shut without him making a sound. If he hadn't looked so utterly thrilled by the proposal she would've worried he was searching for the words to let her down gently.

'Is that a yes?'

'That's a yes to being your husband, yes to being daddy Cal and yes to spending every day of the rest of my life with you. On one condition.' His forehead crinkled and turned his handsome face serious again.

Izzy swallowed, concerned that he might impose some impossible demands, but had to trust that belief she had in him that he would never do anything to hurt her.

'Name it,' she said, feigning a bravery she would need to see her through the next months.

'You get some rest.' He kissed her all too fleetingly on the lips.

Now, that she could do. She snuggled down into the bed, exhaustion washing over her in waves now she'd laid herself bare emotionally, but knowing Cal was sticking with her gave her enough comfort to give in to slumber.

'Where will you be when I wake up?' she mumbled, refusing to let go of his hand as she drifted off to sleep.

'Where I belong. Right here beside you.'

She smiled with the soft pressure of his lips against her cheek and knew everything would turn out fine when she woke up because now she had a future with Cal to look forward to. This family of convenience had become one she was going to cherish for ever.

EPILOGUE

'I NOW PRONOUNCE YOU husband and wife.'

The registrar legally confirmed their commitment to one another, although Cal and Izzy had done that almost a year ago in the hospital.

'I can kiss the bride now, right?'

As if he would've let anyone stop him. Izzy would never tire of letting him either. Being able to kiss Cal any time she pleased was one of the many good things to come her way.

The registrar nodded her approval as Cal dipped his new bride back for a true Hollywood-romance-style kiss, which still had the ability to make Izzy spend the rest of the day walking around in a daze.

A chorus of whoops and cheers rang out from the congregated guests as they finally made their relationship official. They had planned an altogether different wedding from the one currently taking place, but seeing the sea of smiling faces cheering them down the aisle, Izzy was grateful at how things had turned out.

Originally, she'd envisaged a quick, quiet ceremony with no fuss so the twins would be born into a stable relationship but, as Cal had pointed out, they were going to have that regardless of a piece of paper. They'd also decided they didn't need the extra stress of wedding preparations when she already had an increased risk of going into premature labour.

She'd been true to her word and stuck to complete bed rest and Cal had gone above and beyond the duties of a loving partner and father-to-be. He'd taken time off work to play nursemaid as well as crawl into bed to watch movies with her and cook every meal for her to make sure she didn't die of boredom or malnutrition in the run-up to the birth.

That time together had been precious for them as a couple, getting to know each other again minus their baggage. She believed it was a major contributing factor to the babies hanging on until her thirty-fourth week. The amniotic sac had resealed itself after that terrifying episode and, although a little on the small side, their girls had been born healthy and able to come home after just a few days. Then the fun had really started, and those quiet moments together had become few and far between. There was never a dull moment in the Armstrong household now and she was thankful for it.

The extra time since the birth and announcing their intention to get married had given them a chance to share their special day with the important people in their lives. Mac and the guys from work were here to celebrate with them and Cal's sisters had travelled with their families to be with them. Perhaps it wasn't too late for any of them to be a real family.

'I love you, Mrs Armstrong, but I hate to break it to you: I'm leaving you for the other two special girls in my life.' Cal stopped halfway down the aisle and let go of her hand to reach for the beauties who'd caught his eye on the way past.

'Oh, well. It was fun while it lasted.' Izzy knew she could never compare to the other important people in this marriage but for once she was happy to come second in Cal's affections when she was equally enamoured with their daughters.

'Come here, Nelly Belly.' Cal reached for the cute bundle trying to wriggle out of Helen's arms to reach her daddy and Izzy did the same with Nell's sister, Rae. She had her best friend and her husband to thank for the twins' still pristine flower girl outfits as they'd juggled the childcare duties during the ceremony. But neither she nor Cal would be parted from them for longer than necessary. They'd named the girls after Cal's parents, Ray and Eleanor, and Cal was the most devoted father anyone could ever wish for. These girls would be as spoiled and happy as she was with him in their lives.

'Well, husband, I think it's time this family really got the party started. Everyone back to our place for champagne and cake.' Their home was their favourite place in the world and the natural choice for a venue in which to celebrate their big day with friends and family. On this occasion Cal had delegated the cooking to caterers so he could spend as much quality time with her and the girls as possible.

Izzy's heart was so full of love for this man she knew it wouldn't be long before the Armstrong family would be growing again…

* * * * *